This Book is Cursed

Robbie Dorman

This Book is Cursed by Robbie Dorman

www.robbiedorman.com

ISBN-13: 978-1-958768-18-1

Cover design by Bukovero

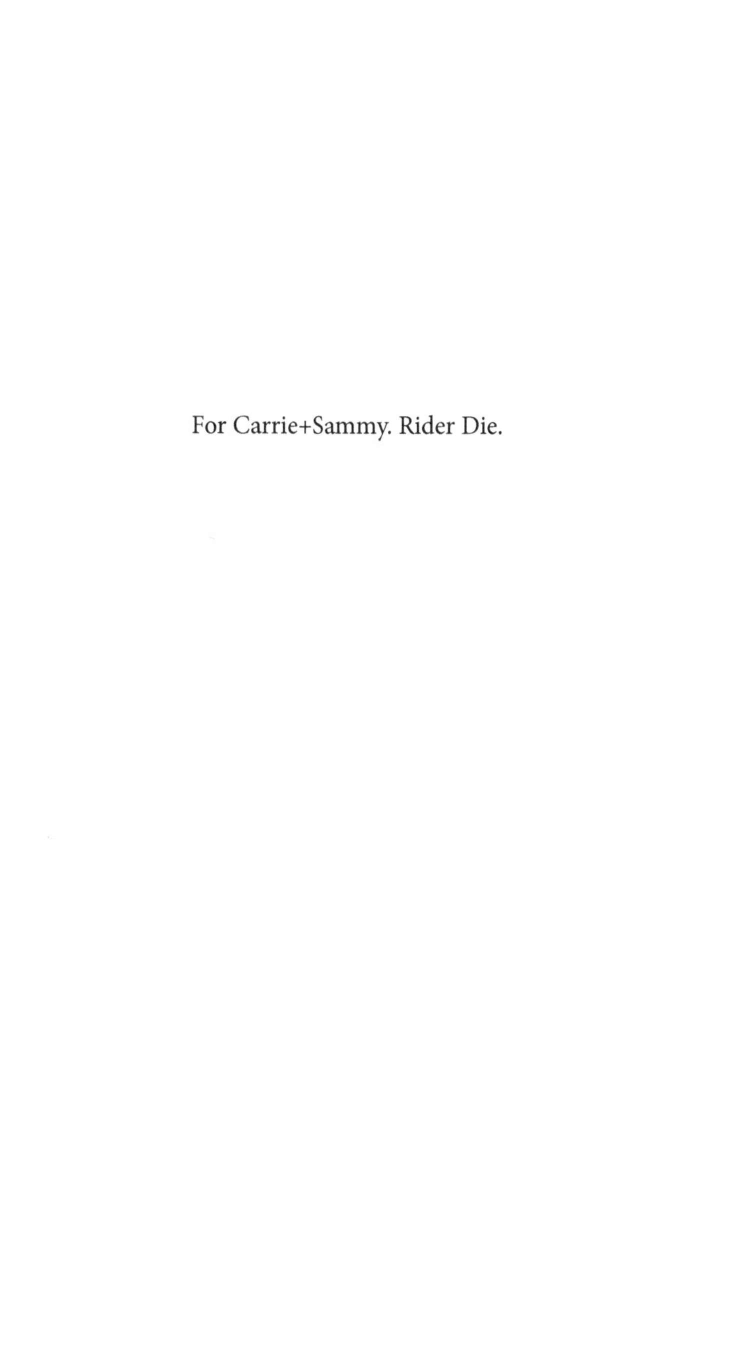

For Carrie+Sammy. Rider Die.

1

Eddie stared at the thin paperback book, clutched in his shaking hand. It was time.

But no, not here. This wasn't the right place. He couldn't read here.

He had kept the book in a safe place, away from the rest of the books, away from the clutter, away from prying eyes and grasping fingers. It was much too valuable, especially if what they said was true. It had been secret, away, in the small safe in the basement, the safe he had bought when the store was almost ready to get off the ground, when he knew he would need somewhere to keep his important paperwork, and cash, and any rare books—

His hips screamed in pain, and he stood up, holding the book in a clammy hand, closing the safe. It felt like any other book, like the thousands that were stacked down here around him.

Deep stacks, that reached to the ceiling, taking up every inch of available space. Books of all types. He had sorted them, back when he thought he would need to, but he had abandoned that, there was no point anymore, no need. They had stacked them down here after he couldn't afford the storage space anymore, and he wouldn't sell them, and he wouldn't throw them away, you didn't throw away books, Eddie couldn't stomach the thought.

"It's sacrilege," muttered Eddie to no one, skirting around the stacks and stacks of books, thousands of books, their musty pages making the basement smell like old paper.

He squeezed the book in his grip, feeling its pliable pages bend, he couldn't lose it. It was his last chance. He had respected its power, he had respected its myth, and had exhausted all his other opportunities.

"Fuckin' bank, won't give a small business a chance," Eddie muttered again, but a little louder, a little venom in his voice. The loan had been promised, he had banked everything on getting that loan. He had picked out the perfect building, just inside downtown, not too small, not too big, and it would have been perfect. Next to the cafe, across the street from the record store. Would have funneled customers right to his shop.

But his contact at the bank left, moved, and the new guy didn't like Eddie, didn't like his chances, and wouldn't take his house as collateral.

And the dream of his bookstore faded.

But Eddie didn't give up. He wouldn't give up, not that easily. Because Eddie loved bookstores, and he loved books.

There were no bookstores where Eddie grew up, not a small mom and pop shop, not a big chain, and nothing in between. Their library was tiny, and filled with old westerns, and romance novels, but still, Eddie was there every day he could get a ride from his mom, until he got a bike, and then rode down there himself, reading anything halfway palatable, earnestly searching for anything interesting. He started with the illustrated editions of classics, but quickly switched to the full, unabridged versions as he grew older, realizing the children's versions were a half step.

But he quickly devoured anything. Literature, westerns, mysteries—but he desperately craved science fiction, fantasy, and horror. When the library acquired something with a dragon on the cover, or a starship, or a monster—Eddie snatched it up as fast as he could.

And the library was great, but as he grew older, and worked on his own, and grew up, and moved out, and could live in a place with a bookstore, and afford books of his own, the thrill of buying a book, of owning a book, overwhelmed him.

And so the collection started.

Eddie didn't think of it as a collection at first. He bought books he wanted to read. And sure, as he entered a comfortable living as an engineer, he could afford many more books than he had time for, as his free time dwindled. But he still wanted to read them. He *would* read them, he told himself.

But with no family, and no spouse, he kept buying. He'd drive to all the used bookstores within a 100 miles, and he'd come home with a car full of books. Any cover that grabbed his attention, regardless of quality.

Eddie's house was soon filled with books, and the storage space became necessary if he would get around his own house. And he had the money. It wasn't a big deal.

That's what he told himself.

And as the collection grew and grew, the thought occurred to him.

What if he opened a bookstore?

His career had stalled, and he had gotten bored with it. The money was good, sure, but he wasn't fulfilled by it, and it always had only served as a means to provide for his book buying.

But once the thought entered his mind, it wouldn't leave. He would start a bookstore. So he geared up for it, buying more and more books, even buying out the entire inventory of multiple stores. He would need the stock.

More storage space, more and more, as the books piled up. But it was okay, it was okay. He would sell those books, and make his money back, and more than that, provide the thing he never had as a child. He would be the place where the book starved populace could come in, and pick up a used paperback for a reasonable price or even sit down in the corner of the store and read it right there, and not even pay for the book, Eddie didn't care, he just wanted that place to exist, an oasis in a desert—

But then everything fell apart, piece by piece.

His job went first. He was in his 50s, and had worked in the same firm for twenty years, and had felt secure there, felt like he would retire there. But a layoff came out of nowhere. And he should have seen the writing on the wall.

And he thought that was a sign, a sign to pursue the bookstore, to make it his full-time job.

But then he fell from a ladder, while hanging Christmas

lights. Medical bills, without insurance.

And the bank decided he wasn't worth the risk of a loan.

And he couldn't afford the storage space anymore.

All he had left was the house. A house filled with books.

Eddie climbed out of the basement, his hips and back screaming with pain. He could deal with it, he could, at least for now. He worried about the future, of trying to climb steps when he was 70, but he had to survive tomorrow first.

The stairs were stacked with books, and he opened the door to the main floor of his house, and all he saw were books. The stacks surrounded him, the inside of the house dark, the stacks blotting out the sunlight from the windows, from the lights overhead.

For most of his life, the books had felt like salvation. He could grab any of them from his shelf. Hold them in his hand, and glory at the cover, at the printing, at the magic that brought an entire world to him, one that he could access at any time, a magic that would have been impossible even a few hundred years ago.

Now, they felt like a prison.

There's a way out. You're holding it.

Eddie looked down again at the book. His guts gnawed at him inside, a nervous anxiousness that he hadn't felt in many years. Was it true, what they said? He doubted it, had doubted it even when he bought it, had spent way too much of his dwindling cash reserves for it—

But if it was true?

If it was true, it was priceless.

Eddie picked his way through his house, working his way past stacks, being careful to not disturb them. The house was cold, the winter settling in, and Eddie didn't have the money to heat the house, not this winter. He would bundle up, and turn on a space heater in his bedroom, on bad nights.

Not for long. Soon, you'll be set.

Eddie dismissed those thoughts. He'd counted chickens before they hatched with his job, with the bookstore, with his health. He wouldn't do it again. The book was just a book, until it proved otherwise.

He snaked his way to the stairs, working his way to the second floor, pain ripping through him, and he grimaced and grit his teeth but kept climbing, holding the book tight in his hand. It was thin, just over a hundred pages, but it felt heavier as he climbed. He wouldn't let go. It was his last hope.

The pain in his back relented as he reached the top step. He pushed past more stacks, lined up in the upstairs hallway, to the room at the end of the hall, all the way opposite from his bedroom.

His shoulder brushed a stack and it wobbled, and he snapped out a hand to steady the stack, before it collapsed, taking the rest of the tenuously stacked books with it. It would take all day to clean up, and Eddie didn't have the energy.

He was getting ahead of himself. The book called to him now, and he told himself, he told himself—

—it's just a book, just a book—

But the promise within was tempting. It would solve everything. He would just need to get to the end.

He reached the door, and opened it, closing it softly behind him, and he could breathe again, letting out a short breath that eased the building tension inside him, the anxiety about what he held, and what waited for him.

The den was decorated sparsely. A plush recliner sat in the corner, a window angled down above it, lighting the room with clean sun. A single small bookshelf stood against the wall. In it, Eddie kept his most precious books. Not the rarest, or the most valuable, but those he loved the most. The books he had read. Books from his childhood, the few he had kept through the years. The ones that had touched him. The ones that meant the most.

He could have used the room to store more books. God knew he needed every square inch he could find, but he refused to touch this room. It was the last piece of solace he had. The final remnant of the life he wanted again.

Here. This is where he would read.

Eddie sat down, the tugging pain in his spine relenting as he eased down into the plush chair. He looked at the book, holding it in two hands. Looking at it, but not opening it. Not yet.

Choose Your Fate: The Mystery of the Sentinel Lodge read the cover, with an illustration of a long hotel corridor, with two creepy children staring from the end. The book looked new, but was otherwise unremarkable.

Eddie had loved the Choose Your Fate books as a child, when he could get his hands on them. He knew there were a lot of them, evidenced by the checklist in the back of every book, listing dozens of titles. Eddie would stare at the list, and wonder what all those books could possibly contain, the adventures you could go on.

Eddie knew now that most of them were filled with mediocre writing that only impressed children, and cliffhanger page turns.

As a child, they were impressive. They were *special.*

But that wasn't true. He just didn't have access. If they had more money, if they lived closer to a bookstore—he would have seen them all.

This book, though, this one *was* special. One of one. A modern rarity. The only one printed.

When he joined book collecting circles, people would whisper about this book. In forums, at used bookstores, at antique fairs, and book markets—once in a while you would see chatter about *The Mystery of the Sentinel Lodge.* One last book, from JP Harmon, before his untimely and gruesome death.

Only one copy ever printed, one he wrote only for himself. Rumors sprung up over the years, growing off each other, about his death, about the nature of the novel, if the book even existed at all.

And most of all, about the book's secret. About the power the book possessed.

It was always dismissed out of hand, by whomever Eddie talked to.

It's impossible, of course. But it's a fun story.

Can you imagine? I'd ask for superpowers. I'd be Superman. Can't be true, though. A story for kids.

I'd love to even see the book. I don't buy for a second that it's magical. Old wives tale.

Because who would admit to believing in such a thing? It's ridiculous. All born up because of the rarity of the book. A single printing, a lone copy, and rumored to be at the dismembered body of Harmon himself.

Eddie doubted the book existed for a long time, but after spending enough money, in enough places, he earned the trust of some collectors, some sellers, and talk about it came up.

Would you be interested?

That was the question, and the matter of price came up, and it was too much, more than Eddie should spend on any one book, even with his well-paying, secure job.

But he said yes. How could he not?

And some months later, he got the call, that his friend Jack, the bookseller in New York, who knew people who knew people who knew people, got his hands on it.

And Eddie handed over the check, a painfully large one, but he had the book. He held it in his hands. Jack only asked that he didn't read it in the store.

"Why?" Eddie had asked.

Jack had smiled, a false smile, one that hid fear. "Just in case."

Eddie had nodded. He had asked a single question before leaving Jack. "Why did they agree to sell it? It's so rare. Did they need the money?"

"I usually don't ask—"

"But—"

"But I did ask." He had smiled. "They only said they didn't need it anymore."

And Eddie held it in his hands, sitting in his plush reading chair, the last refuge he had in his house filled with books.

And of course, at first, he hadn't believed the stories.

It was ridiculous.

Urban legend.

But then he looked into it on his own.

And then he had set it aside. He wanted desperately to

read it. It would solve all his problems.

But he didn't. He exhausted all his other opportunities.

And now, only this was left.

He rubbed at the thin cover of the small book.

He opened it, and started reading.

Your breath catches in your lungs as the chill air enters them. You stand outside of the Sentinel Lodge, six stories tall, staring down at you. The Rockies surround you, mountains towering high.

A voice startles you.

"You must be my new assistant caretaker," said the voice, and you turn to see a man who looks to be in his 50s, with graying hair and cold eyes. They are squinted against the glare of the sun off the snowpack.

"I am," you say.

"I'm Carl Douglas," he says, and he extends a hand. You reach out and shake it, his hand big, enveloping yours, and he smiles as he squeezes.

"Nice to meet you," he said. "Follow me inside."

TURN TO PAGE 3

Eddie turned the page, and continued reading. His heart thumped against his rib cage, and his stomach ached.

He read, following the story, his story, as he met the caretaker Carl. As Carl warned him against wandering the grounds of the lodge at night. As he disobeyed. But he hadn't hit an ending yet. He could find his way to the true ending, a happy ending.

His eyes danced over the words, carefully dissecting every one. He chose to leave his room in the dark. He went right down the hall, and up the stairs, not down. If he would solve the mystery of the Sentinel Lodge, he would have to confront it head on.

But as Eddie walked through the dark nighttime hallways of the Sentinel Lodge, he didn't notice his house transforming.

The walls shifted, the door changed. The wallpaper inside the room morphed to wood paneling, and even the smell of paper and pulp turned into the scent of a musty lodge, of fireplace and melting snow.

Eddie reached the end of the page. He stood in front of the door to room 317.

TO ENTER ROOM 317, TURN TO PAGE 54
TO TURN BACK, TURN TO PAGE 72

Eddie's heart raced, and he finally looked up, and saw where he was. He fought every instinct to get up. To leave the book behind, and to race from his room. To hope his house would be his house beyond this door.

But he stayed seated, the book in his hands. He knew, knew somehow, that leaving the book behind now would seal his fate.

He turned to page 54.

His eyes danced over the sparse words on the page. But he saw the words at the end well before he finished reading.

THE END

No no no no—

A wailing sound of sadness and grief and horror echoed

from outside his door.

No, please, let me go back, let me start over—

His door creaked open, and there were no stacks of books on the other side, only the long hallways of the Sentinel Lodge.

But then he saw her. Her face contorted in sorrow, in sadness. She wailed, wailed even as she approached. Tears poured from her, an impossible torrent of liquid pooling around her feet.

"You abandoned me! You became someone else!" she screamed, her voice haggard, coming out as wails of sorrow.

"No, no—" he begged, but she charged, flying toward him at a speed he didn't expect, and her ghastly hand reached inside him, and he felt her cold fingers wrap around his heart and *squeeze—*

"P-please," he forced out, but she squeezed harder, and his vision faded.

I only wanted a bookstore was the last thought that passed through his mind before his heart collapsed in his chest, and the book fell from his hands to the floor.

2

BEEP

BEEP

BEEP

Annie Maddox worked through the stack of paperbacks, scanning them through the point of sale system. One after the other. Brad had found a storage locker full of them at a steep discount, sold by the pound.

Most of them were dollar books, but a handful of them were rare or vintage, and in good enough shape to sell for a decent value.

BEEP

Her phone emitted a tiny noise after each scan, her camera working as the scanner. She would have loved a barcode scanner, but they were expensive. It was on the wishlist for her fledgling bookstore, at the end of the strip mall, next door to the pizza palace, which was next to the head shop, which was next to the Chinese delivery place. All of them had existed for a couple of years, which made them successful, at least in the terms of Ridgefield, at least in the terms of the strip mall.

Annie had looked up the rental history of this space, before they had committed to it, and it served as a graveyard of small businesses who thought maybe, just maybe, Ridgefield could support them.

They had all miscalculated. Annie hoped that The Book Barn would be different.

Hope was the key word.

But the only reason she was scanning in paperback books into their inventory system was because the shop was dead, empty for the last few hours, since they had opened at 11. It was almost the holiday season, and she would have bet they would have gotten some Christmas shopping traffic, something, she had set out and decorated to appeal to the gift shopper, even put out recommendation cards, but nothing, no bites—

The bell rang as the front door opened, and there was a burst of excitement—*a customer*—

"Hi Annie," said Tim, as he forced his way through the heavy swinging door. Tim was small, only 5 foot tall, and skinny as a rail, a thirteen-year-old kid who had stopped in once a week since they'd opened, but had bought nothing. He browsed a lot, and Annie saw the marvel in his face as he picked up different books, and stared at their covers, and devoured the blurbs on the back, and talked to her quite a bit.

But Tim didn't have any money. She was sure if he had it, he would have gone home laden with books every time he came into the shop.

But he hadn't bought a thing.

You made this store for him.

And she had. For kids who needed books in their lives, for adults who wanted a real place, in their area, that could provide a feeling of community, and give them the books a big box store wouldn't.

Not that there was a big box store nearby, anyway. The nearest Barnes and Noble was an hour's drive away. Sure, you could order them off Amazon, but it wasn't the same. You couldn't feel a book, buying online, couldn't pick it up, and feel the weight, touch the hard spine, or flip your thumb through old pages.

The smell of a bookstore. The smell of paper, and ink, and the feeling of safety and happiness present surrounded by a world of potentiality.

It didn't matter that Tim couldn't spend any money. The bookstore was still there for him.

"Hi, Tim," said Annie, putting the stack aside. "How are you?"

"I'm okay," he said. "Glad to be out of school."

"Winter break?"

"Yeah," he said. "Free until next year." He stared at their genre wall, shelves filled with mystery and sci-fi and fantasy and horror. A mixture of used, gently used, and new books. He grabbed something off the shelf, a pocket paperback, and stared at it, flipped through it, and looked at the back.

He returned it to its spot. He did this for a few more minutes until he made his way to the counter.

"I was wondering—"

"You were wondering what, Tim?" asked Annie.

"Are you hiring? For part time work?" asked Tim. "During the holidays? I'm old enough now, and if I worked here, I could read all the books I wanted, it'd be awesome—"

"Sorry," said Annie. "I can't justify hiring anyone right now. But if we do, I'll let you know. I wish I had that problem."

"Oh," said Tim, and Annie saw the look of disappointment in his eyes. "Are people not coming in?"

"It's been slow."

"I've been telling everyone I know," said Tim. "I want to buy stuff, I do, I just don't—"

"I know," said Annie. "It's alright. Telling people about us is a big help." She smiled. "Read anything good lately?"

"I read a new Asimov from the library!" said Tim, suddenly excited again. "I think it was Foundation."

"Oh, wow," said Annie. "That's a big one. Did you enjoy it?"

"Yeah," said Tim, his eyes lighting up. "I've never read anything else like it."

"Hmm," said Annie. She stepped out from around the counter and walked over to the genre wall, moving to their patchwork collection of SFF. She wanted more, she wanted more of *everything*, but they couldn't afford to stock all the historically important sci-fi, and all the new science fiction that pushed past the canon. But for their resources, they had a good selection. It didn't hurt that old science fiction paperbacks could be had cheaply, if one knew where to look.

She found Asimov, the three Foundation books in row. She's sure they had more paperbacks in storage, but these were the ones in the nicest condition. A few dollars a piece. She took them off the shelf.

"We have all three," she said. "There are other connected books, but these three are plenty good for now."

"I—I don't have the money for them," said Tim. "I know I say that every time, and I've asked my parents, but they just don't—"

"Take them," said Annie. "No charge."

"What? Really?" said Tim. He didn't put out his hands. Annie held out the three books, in a stack.

"Yes."

"I—I can't do that," said Tim. "I can't just—"

"When you have some extra money, will you come back and pick up something?"

"Yeah, of course."

"Then take them," said Annie, practically thrusting the books at Tim. Tim finally grabbed the stack in his hands.

"I—thank you," he said, meeting Annie's eyes for a second and then looking away. His cheeks were turning pink.

"I have only one other request," said Annie. His eyes met hers again. "I want to know what you think after you read them."

"O-okay," said Tim. He tucked the books under his arm, clasping them tightly. "I can do that. Thank you again."

"Thank you for spreading the word," said Annie, smiling, and then Tim left, looking down at the books as he walked out the door, the bell ringing.

Annie made a mental note to replace the books with some of their back stock, and returned behind the counter only for the bell to ring again. She looked up with interest.

Two customers in a row? Maybe things were picking up.

But she recognized the face as it entered. It wasn't a customer. It was Brad.

"Was that Tim?" he asked, walking in with a box cradled in his arms.

"Yes, back again," said Annie.

"Did he finally buy something?" asked Brad, dropping the box on the counter.

"He got the three Asimov Foundation books," said Annie, not making eye contact with Brad.

"Mmmhmm," muttered Brad, studying Annie. "And let me guess. He did not purchase those books."

Annie didn't answer.

"Annie—"

"He's a sad sack every time he comes in here, and—"

"Annie—"

"He loves to read, Brad," said Annie, finally meeting his eyes. "So, I gave him the books."

Brad still looked at her, his face a question mark. He took a breath. "How are we going to make money if we give away our inventory?"

"He's a good kid, Brad," said Annie. "I didn't start this bookstore to make money. I did it to give people access to books they otherwise wouldn't have. To spread the joy of reading."

"I did it for both reasons," said Brad, after a beat.

"It's nine bucks," said Annie. "If it comes down to nine dollars, win or lose, we may have miscalculated, one way or the other. We probably have half a dozen copies of those books."

Brad only stared, his eyebrow cocked.

"Are you telling me not to give away nearly worthless paperback books to youths who love to read?"

Brad finally broke his gaze. "No, I'm not telling you that."

"So you agree," said Annie, smiling.

He shook his head. "This place is going to collapse and I'm going to have to crawl back to Worsham, on my hands and knees, begging for a job."

"They'd kill to have you back."

"Yeah, they probably would," said Brad. "Please don't give away books to people who actually *can* pay."

"Scout's honor," said Annie, raising her hand.

"You weren't a scout."

"I've been found out," said Annie. "What's in the box?"

"Some finds," said Brad. "I went down to Hollisford. There was an estate sale there. Got in early, and grabbed some stuff we can flip for easy money. A few first editions, a couple of rare paperbacks in good condition." He pulled them out of the box and stacked them on the counter. "Only cost a few hundred, and could net us a few thousand, after everything is said and done."

Annie sighed quietly, looking at the stacks of books. Brad looked back at her.

"What? What are you sighing about?"

"It's nothing."

"Don't nothing me," said Brad. "Out with it."

"I know we have to make money—"

"But—"

"But this feels kinda—I don't know—gross."

Brad rolled his eyes with an exaggerated motion. "We are booksellers. This is what we do. We sell books."

"I don't want to be a vulture," said Annie. "Feasting off the death of some poor soul, taking their books, and reselling them at a markup."

"Hey, we have good prices," said Brad. "I don't want to sit on books for years. We keep things moving."

"It's not that."

"You mean, it's not giving an underprivileged youth some free books, but actually making money by doing business?"

"Well—yes."

"That's why I'm in charge of this part," said Brad. "And you're in charge of this." Brad gestured around them. "You don't have to get your hands dirty in this filthy game I play." He smiled and steeped his fingers menacingly. "Look at this cover!" He held out a beautifully illustrated fantasy novel.

"Is it valuable?"

"No, not really," said Brad. He smiled. "This one's for me."

"Ah, I see how it is," said Annie. "I can't give away books, but you can buy for yourself on company time."

"Exactly," said Brad, smirking. "And yes, in a perfect world, we wouldn't have to scavenge through estate sales and resort to Instagram and eBay. But we don't live in a perfect world. We live in a world where we are going to have to scratch and claw to survive as a bookstore in a small town. And I don't want to go back to Worsham. I want the same thing you want, to make this place an institution. And if we have to go buy some poor dead person's book and sell them online to do that, I can handle it for the both of us. If it helps, this box will buy us a lot of books to give away to Tim and kids like him."

Annie took a deep breath. "You're right. I know you're right."

"Man," said Brad. "I should have recorded that. You can

play it at my funeral."

"You might be getting ahead of yourself," said Annie.

"You've seen what I eat," said Brad. "There's no way I outlive you. But please, when you eulogize me, tell them all about this momentous occasion."

Annie shook her head. "You're horrible. How does Gabby put up with you?"

"See, that's the trick," said Brad. He leaned in. "She actually likes it."

"I don't know how."

Brad smiled. "It's my ineffable charm. Simple as that. Speaking of—"

"What?"

"I need your help this weekend."

"Help with what?"

"There's an estate auction, about an hour away," said Brad. "I've got a tip that there's some good stuff in there."

"What about the store?"

"It's in the morning," said Brad. "We might have to open slightly later, but it won't be a big deal."

"You just said I won't have to get my hands dirty."

"Well, unfortunately, it's just us," said Brad. "And if we're lucky, there will be way too many books for me to handle on my own. This guy apparently has thousands and thousands, all stacked up in his house. Some rare stuff, too."

"A hoarder?" asked Annie.

"I don't know," said Brad. "But I trust my source. He hasn't led me wrong yet. And there might be gold in them thar hills."

"Can I really say no?"

"I mean, you can," said Brad. "I could ask Gabby, but we'd

have to get a sitter for Buddy, and I—"

"I'll do it," said Annie. "But I get to pick the music on the drive."

Brad sighed. "I'll prepare myself for hours of Taylor Swift."

"Oh, I don't want to hear it," said Annie. "I saw your wrapped from last year. She was what, number three on your list?"

"I'm sure I don't know what you're talking about," said Brad, still smirking. "Bright and early, Saturday. I'll grab us some breakfast tacos."

"Finally, saying the right things."

"You won't regret it," said Brad. "Guarantee we'll get the find of a lifetime."

3

"So, how does this all work?" asked Annie.

They sat in front of a two-story house in the late morning. The air was brisk, but the sun shone brightly, and made the weather outside tolerable. Still, Annie pulled her hood over her head, and cinched it tight.

Annie and Brad sat in metal folding chairs on the front lawn along with a few dozen others. A quick count put the number of chairs at 64, but they weren't all occupied. A small podium stood in front of them.

"It's just an auction," said Brad. "The auctioneer will call out a lot number, give us a brief description, and then take bids."

"I thought this was going to an estate sale."

"It is."

"But it's an auction."

"Sometimes they do sales at fixed prices, sometimes they do auctions," said Brad. "They probably think there's some demand for some items here, so they chose to do an auction. All you need is two people who really want something, and it can drive up the price."

"What are we looking for?" asked Annie. "Anything you have your eye on?"

"Not specifically," said Brad. "The lots don't have every book listed. They put these together quickly, so there is an element of gambling. You're never sure what you're going to get."

"Then why are we here?"

"Because we can get a lot of books for very, very cheap," said Brad. "Some of these lots will have thousands of books, penny on the pound. We just have to pick our spots, and we'll take home a lot of books for very little cost."

"Doesn't seem like there's many people here."

"No," said Brad. "For our benefit."

"Do you know what happened to the guy?" asked Annie. She stared at the two-story house in front of them. It was a nice mid-century home, painted yellow, with white shutters. It looked perfectly normal from the outside.

"No idea," said Brad. "My source told me the guy was a big collector. That's all I know. But that probably means a lot of hidden gems, even among the more common lots. And maybe even some real rare stuff. But I don't know if we'll have the capital to get the more valuable lots." Brad glanced around. "I'm guessing we're not alone in trying to snag some of the rarer books."

Annie looked. There were a variety of people here. Her

eyes flitted around, landing on some of them, before she locked eyes with a well-dressed woman, in a tailored suit, small, her eyes intense. She stared at Annie, and Annie looked away, and turned back around.

"Still feels gross," said Annie. "I feel like carrion."

"Anything that isn't sold will probably be thrown away," said Brad. "Better with us than in a landfill."

"Fair enough," said Annie, sighing. "How much longer before this thing starts? It's past eleven—"

"Probably giving stragglers time to arrive," said Brad. "But I doubt there'll be anyone else—oh, here's the auctioneer."

He wore a suit, and had stood off to the side under a small canopy with another man, presumably whoever was in charge of the auction.

"Alright, folks, nice to see you all here. We'll begin with the book lots, and then continue to the rest of the material goods, and then the furniture, last, okay? If you win a lot, please remain until the end of the auction."

He paused, looked around, and then began. "Alright, starting with Lot One, all the books stored in the curio cabinet. This lot includes paperbacks and hardcovers, less than a hundred books. Bidding will begin at one hundred dollars."

The action came quickly then, with someone behind them immediately bidding, and the auctioneer calling out subsequent bids. Brad seemed poised to bid, but soon the bids went over $500, and then over a $1000, and Brad put his small paddle down into his lap.

"Too rich for our blood," said Brad.

Annie glanced back again as the bid went higher and higher, $100 at a time. There were three people bidding, a man, and two women, one of whom she locked eyes with earlier. As the bid soared over $5000, one woman dropped out, with a man and woman remaining.

But they didn't stop. The bidding continued, up and up. Soon, it was over ten thousand dollars.

"Do they know something we don't?" Annie whispered, leaning toward Brad.

"My friend had some info," said Brad. "But there's no way in hell we can afford this, sight unseen. Those two though—they might have some inside information. It's alright. We can wait for the other lots. Still a lot of value in them."

Annie expected one of the two of them to stop, but the price only rose. $12K, $15K, and then as it neared $20K, there was a pause. Annie glanced back and saw she wasn't the only one doing so. Everyone was taking in the show. The man, nearer to her, had the leading bid, and the well-dressed woman had hesitated to raise hers. Her intense eyes were closed, thinking through something.

Annie looked at the man, who looked normal enough, his only distinguishing feature a small scar that curled alongside his right eyebrow. The well-dressed woman sat behind him, but his eyes were cast to the side, looking at her through his peripheral vision. A smirk shone through his poker face.

"Nineteen, nineteen, do I have nineteen five? Asking for nineteen five, nineteen five." He looked around, but his eyes were really only for the well-dressed woman, who finally opened her eyes, but did not raise her paddle. "High bid nineteen—going once—going twice—gone! Sold for nineteen thousand."

The smirk on the man with the scar grew into a wide

smile, and he pumped his fist once, softly.

"That's the most I've seen a lot go for," said Brad, quietly.

"Onto Lot 2. All the books found in the kitchen, yes, the kitchen. All paperbacks, loosely stacked. Roughly one thousand books. Starting bid is $50."

Hands started going up now, Brad's included. But as the prices rose, Brad fell off.

"We'll wait for the later book lots," said Brad. "They'll be cheaper. Doubt there's a difference in quality."

Annie only nodded. Brad understood this better than her. She eyed the man with the scar. He sat, still smiling, but wasn't bidding on any of the bigger lots. He had gotten what he came for. She looked back at the well-dressed woman, but she was already gone.

Guess there was no reason to stick around.

The auction continued, with lots seemingly built only around where the books were in the home. Annie looked again at the house, trying to imagine those books, stacked up in each room inside. Navigating the house, slim tunnels built around the stacks.

But Brad's instincts were right. As the auction continued, the prices steadily dropped, until lots were going only for $50 to $100. Brad started snapping them up, getting one from the downstairs, and buying everything that was upstairs. Their final price was only $300, winning 6 lots.

"Jackpot, buddy," he said, smiling.

"That happened fast."

"They're pros," said Brad. "They'll work through all the furniture, and miscellaneous stuff. I'm sure some people are here for that. After it's all done, we'll settle up and grab our loot."

Annie grimaced at the word "loot" but said nothing, and Brad was right. There was heavy interest in the furniture, in everything, and little was left with no bids.

After the event was over, they settled up with the folks in charge, and a helper led them to their lots, already boxed up, dozens and dozens of small boxes.

"Jesus," said Annie. "That's a lot of books. Good thing we brought the truck. You think it'll all fit?"

"We'll make it fit," said Brad. "Let's get started."

They grabbed the cart and the dolly and got to work, loading up box after box into the U-Haul they had gotten for the day. Annie had questioned the need for something so big, but it was a good call. It would have taken multiple trips in her SUV. They stacked waist-high boxes of books all the way to the back of the truck. Even in the cool air, Annie and Brad were both sweating and panting as they moved the last few loads.

As they loaded, Annie noticed a woman watching them from a distance. She looked to be in her 50s, maybe older. She stood on the sidewalk, staring at them.

"You see her?" asked Annie, as she passed Brad.

"See who?"

"The woman," said Annie. "Out on the sidewalk. Been watching us the entire time."

"It's a small neighborhood, lots of looky loos."

"But she's only been watching us."

"I wouldn't worry about it," said Brad. "Once we load up, we'll never see this place again."

Annie surveyed the boxes as they finished.

"There has to be five thousand books in here," said Annie. "How many of them can we sell?"

"I don't know," said Brad. "There's only a few hundred worth anything. But there will almost certainly be a few worth more than we think, and that's where we'll make our money. And even then—"

"Did you get all of Eddie's books?" asked a voice, suddenly. Annie jumped. She looked to the source, and it was the woman who had been watching them. She had walked up to the truck without Annie noticing. Close up, the woman was certainly in her 60s, with hair dyed jet black. She stared at the two of them, her eyes dancing between them.

"Uh—no," said Brad. "There were other lots we didn't get. We probably got most of them, though."

"I'm Betty," she said. "I live next door. I found Eddie."

"Oh—I'm sorry."

"He was too young," said Betty. "Much too young."

"I—"

"But did you get the books upstairs?" asked Betty.

"Y—yes," said Brad. This little old lady didn't pose a threat to them, but Annie sensed the unease in Brad. She felt it too.

"Will you take care of them?" she asked.

"Take care of the books?" asked Annie. The woman's eyes were dark, nearly as dark as her hair, and Annie had trouble maintaining eye contact.

"Yes, yes, the books," said Betty. "Eddie cared about his books. More than anything."

"We'll certainly try our best," said Brad. "We run a bookstore. We love books, too."

"That's good, that's good," she said. She looked away once, her face turning dark. "I talked to the man with the scar. I asked him, too. He laughed at me."

"I'm sorry—"

"He laughed about taking care of books," said Betty. "What's happened to people nowadays?" She paused, and the air was silent. She broke it. "Eddie would want his books taken care of. That's all."

"We'll take care of them, ma'am," said Annie. "I promise. We'll get them to good homes."

"Good, good," said Betty, some sort of comfort finally showing on her face, the coldness and aloofness finally breaking. She moved closer to Annie, and Annie had to force herself to stand her ground, as the woman drew within a foot.

"You have it, you know," she said, her voice low, almost a growl.

"Have what?" asked Annie.

"When I found Eddie, he was holding a book," she said. "I put it with the rest. It felt right. It's somewhere in there." She gestured toward the stacks of boxes.

"He was holding a book?" asked Brad.

"When he died," said Betty. "It felt right. They all belonged together." She stared at Annie, and smiled. "And now you have it."

4

BEEP

It felt right.

BEEP

They all belonged together.

BEEP

You have it, you know.

BEEP

Annie scanned in the books, one by one, box by box. She would take a book out of the box, look at it, examine it, and inspect it. What genre was it? Was it new to her? What condition was it in, and was it in the system?

She felt the familiar weight of each book, the aged, yellowed paper. The slight texture of the page underneath her fingerprints. The faint smell of must. When the shop was slow, she enjoyed sorting through new books, even if it was maddeningly tedious.

But a thought lingered. A question asked about every book passed.

Was this the book?

Was this the book he held as he died?

Eddie, is what the woman had said. His name was Eddie.

She held a thriller, a spy novel, countless westerns, and every time she scanned one, every book she glanced at, the thought was there.

Was this the book Eddie clasped as he died?

She pushed the thought out of her head, and continued to scan, book after book. Any first printings or books in excellent quality she put aside. Anything falling apart, she separated as well. The huge amount that fell between would be judged later. Brad would follow up on this work and check online, to see if there was high demand for any of them.

It was tedious, but it had worked so far, keeping them in the black, even as customers were slow to discover the shop.

Annie scanned the books, going through, box by box. They had picked up nearly a hundred boxes at the estate auction, but she made quick work of them. It helped that a lot of the books were unsellable, in such a condition that she wouldn't even give them away, either the covers ripped off, or obviously missing pages. Those were easy to diagnose and saved her time.

But no matter how much she pushed it away, the words of Betty returned. The question if each book was the last one Eddie ever touched.

And as she scanned, and battled with her thoughts, and tried to force the hesitation away as her hands grazed each page, the question of the value of these books persisted. Old paperbacks, printed on cheap paper, sold for a dollar or less originally, originally mass produced, and now valuable, simply because of the poor quality of the print, of being treated as disposable.

But what else added value, aside from rarity? Aside from a good cover and a pulpy story?

Was there value in a book being the last one someone read? Someone touched?

The book that touched death? That felt it?

Did that make it worth more?

Was that a value add?

She scanned them, one by one, sorting them into the appropriate piles and stacks. A handful of customers came and interrupted her, but largely she worked without pause.

But every book she touched brought the question of if it was Eddie's last.

Hundreds and then thousands of books slid under her fingers, and she examined each one.

BEEP

BEEP

BEEP

And then she picked one up, looked at the cover. It was in great shape. Frankly, it looked brand new, a choose your own adventure book titled *Choose Your Fate: The Mystery of the Sentinel Lodge.*

What is this?

They had encountered choose your own adventure books before. There were a hundreds of them, and they had a huge inventory. She hadn't seen this one before, though.

She scanned it in.

No result.

What?

She scanned again. Still no result.

Maybe a problem with the barcode. She manually searched for the title.

No result.

She tried different phrases from the title, and then finally searched the author, JP Harmon. She recognized his name from other Choose Your Fate books they had, and the database had them all, and she sorted by alphabetical, scrolling to where the title should be. But it wasn't there.

"Weird," she muttered.

She examined the book again. The cover was good, if slightly unsettling, obviously inspired by The Shining. Two creepy children stood, staring, at the end of a long hotel corridor, with patterned carpeting.

To the internet she went.

And what she found was nothing. Well, not nothing.

But nothing concrete.

JP Harmon was all over the place, easy to find him. They had other Harmon books, but Annie had never thought to look him up. Turns out Harmon was a pen name for a guy named Mike Sullivan, who published a lot of children's books under many pen names.

His Wikipedia entry was sparse, with most of the information under the heading *Controversy Surrounding Death.*

What the hell?

Annie clicked. Harmon had died under mysterious circumstances, murdered by an assailant never caught, viciously attacked with multiple lacerations to the back, some reports saying he was hacked to pieces.

No murderer ever caught. No murder weapon ever found. With no evidence, Harmon's death was declared unsolved.

Well, that didn't get her any closer to the book.

She repeated her searching strategy for the title online and eventually got only some scattered postings on a handful of forums.

Has anyone heard of a JP Harmon CYOA book called The Sentinel Lodge?

The top reply read *An urban legend. No known copies available anywhere. Think it originated from a press release from the publisher which had a listing of upcoming works, but Harmon died before it came out. If it exists, doubt we'll ever see it. My guess is Harmon never finished it, so they scrubbed it.*

Annie looked back at the book in her hand. It existed. She could see that much. But there was no information in the ISBN database, and no word of it existing online.

A rush of excitement suddenly hit Annie, of realization.

This book does exist, and we have the only copy!

She stared at it now. This must be the proof copy, or something, right before Harmon died, and they didn't release it because of his death.

Was it worth a lot? A one-off book by a big publisher had to be worth something—but it was a choose your own adventure book. Was there a market for those? There had to be, right?

Brad would know. He had contacts with booksellers and collectors. He would know if someone would want it.

Annie set it aside. Brad would be in later in the day, and she'd ask him. He'd have an answer. She got back to work scanning in books, but her thoughts never left the one of a kind choose your own adventure book.

A lot fewer books were scanned until Brad came in just under an hour later, Annie distracted by her thoughts of the lottery ticket that sat on the counter.

Brad came in, carrying another box of books.

"Do you ever stop buying?" asked Annie.

"Takes money to make money," said Brad, setting the box down on the counter. "Anything good?"

"I'm glad you asked," said Annie. She grabbed the thin paperback and handed it over. "I found this."

Brad grabbed it, glanced at it. "Ah, Choose Your Fate. JP Harmon. Had a few of these growing up. Not as many as the proper choose your own adventure books, but I had a few. Absolutely loved them, even if looking back, they were a bit simple. It's in good shape."

"I thought you'd have a bigger reaction."

"Should I?" asked Brad. "I mean, it is in good shape, but these books are a dime a dozen. Might get twenty for it."

Annie smiled. For once, she knew more about the rarity of a book than Brad. "Not that one," said Annie. "That's one of a kind."

"Why?"

Annie told him, telling him everything she had found online.

Brad listened, his eyes narrowed, as he digested the news. A slim smile grew on his face.

"A proper mystery," said Brad, after Annie had finished her spiel. He considered the book. "Truly rare."

"As far as we know," said Annie. "You think your contacts will have any info on it?"

"Hmm," said Brad. "I don't know. Also not sure how many people I want to know we have this."

"What do you mean?"

"If this really is the only copy," said Brad. "Then it's incredibly valuable, and something we wouldn't sell ourselves. We'd probably let one of the big auction houses handle it, like Sotheby's or someone similar."

"Won't they take a cut?"

"Yes," said Brad. "But they'll also handle payment and security and insurance and a dozen other things someone with the money to spend on this would want. Things we can't provide. And once word gets out that we have this, we might start getting unwanted attention. We should probably get a safe deposit box, or something similar, to hold on to things like this. Hell, I might go get one now."

"How much do you think it's worth?"

"Hard to say," said Brad. "All it takes is two different collectors, with enough money, and a bidding war could drive up the price quite high, like yesterday—" Brad stopped, and looked at the book again. "I wonder."

"You wonder what?"

"I wonder if those two with the deep pockets were fishing for this."

"At the estate auction? Do you think they thought this would be in the rare book lot?"

"Impossible to know for sure, but I'd bet they'd heard word of a one of a kind book in that poor man's collection, and were willing to spend big on it. Maybe to keep. Maybe to resell."

"But it wasn't," said Annie. "It was lumped in with all these other paperbacks. Maybe Eddie didn't know what he had."

"Maybe," said Brad. He stared at the book. Annie glanced at him. He was holding something back.

"What are you thinking?"

"I'm thinking about that woman. The neighbor."

Annie's earlier thoughts flooded back in. The last book Eddie read. Then it all clicked, and she looked at Choose Your Fate, and then at Brad.

"You don't think—"

Brad nodded. "It adds up. Eddie takes out the rarest book from his collection, and goes upstairs to read. He passes away with it in his hands, and that woman, and the estate company, don't know the difference between what is rare and what isn't. To them, it's just a paperback choose your own adventure book, like I said, a dime a dozen. It gets lumped in with all this mass printed stuff, and we end up winning the auction."

"And the guys fighting over the rare stuff don't get their white whale."

"It's the luck of the draw," said Brad. "I won't say I'm upset. This might buy us a lot of time. Hell, we might able to buy our own location, if there's enough demand. Books like this, with the backstory it has, and it's rarity, might get us six figures."

"I can't imagine," said Annie. "I don't want to get our hopes up."

"You know what they say, about the number of chickens, before they've hatched. Still, I am going to get us a safety deposit box, and put it in there, until we know what we're doing with it. I'll talk to some people at some auction houses, and see what their process is, and how they feel about the book." He held it in his hand. "This little thing."

"Hard to think it's worth so much."

"There might not be another copy on Earth," said Brad. "Did you read it?"

"No," said Annie. "I didn't want to damage it."

"Smart enough," said Brad. "But I am tempted. I never found my way out of these things. I always wanted to see every ending."

"They still make them, I think."

"Oh, I know," said Brad. "But I do hold a certain nostalgia for it." Brad's thumb went to the edge of the paper and fanned over the pages.

"Going to give it a shot?" asked Annie. "Reading through it one time probably won't hurt. We do need to verify what's inside."

"No time like the present," said Brad, but then the bell on the door rang, and a man entered.

Annie recognized him, and Brad must have as well, because he immediately slid the book across the counter over to her, and she put it underneath.

The man was at the auction. The man with the scar, who had bid nearly twenty thousand dollars for a lot that surely was meant to contain their book.

5

The man smiled as he walked up to the two of them. As he approached, the scar was undeniable, nor the fact this was the same man from the auction. The scar set him apart, but aside from that, he could be any other white man in his mid-30s, with brown hair, and slight stubble. He wore nondescript clothes, which looked like they could be from anywhere.

"I'm glad I wasn't led astray," he said, as he approached, stopping short of both of them.

"Excuse me?" asked Annie.

"A friend told me that two of the winning bidders from the auction ran their own bookstore, and it was quite a hike to get here. But here you are."

"You could have called," said Brad.

"Ah, I could have," said the man. "But I didn't, and here I am."

A silence settled between them for a moment. "Well, can we help you?" asked Annie, finally.

"Oh, I'm sorry," he said. He extended a hand. "I'm Andrew Fleming. Collector of rare books and antiquities, and well, anything else that catches my eye."

Brad hesitated for a second and then shook his hand. "Brad. And this is Annie." Andrew shook Brad's hand, and then extended his hand to Annie as well. She shook it awkwardly over the counter. His hand was a little clammy, his grip loose.

"We saw your big bid at the estate auction," said Annie.

"Yes," said Andrew. "Yes, I had a little competition. I hadn't expected that, but oh well, it is the game I choose to play. Ultimately, I won the bid."

"All the rare books, correct?" asked Brad.

"Oh yes," said Fleming. "A lot of rare finds, of which I was glad to add to my collection. But unfortunately, the one I was specifically looking for was not there. Which brings me to my reason for visiting you fine folks."

"Is that right?" asked Brad. Annie eyed him. Fleming was here for the Choose Your Fate book, assuredly. Their hunch was right about him. But she remembered Brad's words. If they wanted a high price, they needed a bidding war. Should they tell Fleming the truth?

"Oh, yes," said Fleming. "I've been asking around, with all my contacts. Tracking down the different buyers. None of the others have had the book. You're my last stop. You also bought the largest lot of books in total."

"Well, we did get a bunch of them," said Brad. "Which

one are you looking for?"

Fleming eyed him, considering him. Testing his words. Annie watched. She didn't want to reveal anything. She'd let Brad play the game.

"It's a part of the choose your own adventure series called Choose Your Fate. The Mystery of the Sentinel Lodge, by JP Harmon." His eyes were locked on Brad.

"Ah, the Choose Your Fate books," said Brad. "Read them a bunch as a kid. But weren't they mass printed? Couldn't be worth that much. Certainly not thousands of dollars."

"See, that's where you're wrong," said Fleming. "This was a special printing."

"A special printing?" asked Brad. "A one-off?"

"Something like that," said Fleming. "You wouldn't have happened to find it, while you've been scanning in all those books?"

Brad eyed him right back. "Something like that would be worth a pretty penny."

"Oh, assuredly," said Fleming. "The money, well, it isn't the problem. Much like at the auction, I'm willing to pay what it takes. I really just want this specific book."

"Pay what it takes?" asked Brad. "How much is that?"

Fleming smirked, a small upturn of his lip. "I would want to verify the book before I discuss dollar figures." Another silence hung there for a moment, and Brad's mind spun, and he turned to her, his eyes meeting hers. Fleming wanted the book.

She looked back at him, asking him a question with her eyes.

Do we really want to do this?

He stared back, and made a slight gesture with his face.

It told her *I've got this.* Annie swallowed down the doubt she had and reached to where she had hid the book beneath the counter. She slid it over to Brad, and he grabbed the slim paperback.

Annie watched Fleming's face, and it lit up as he saw the book, the distinctive cover and typeface treatment on all the Choose Your Fate books.

"You *do* have it," said Fleming, smiling. His eyes went to the book, and only the book in Brad's hands. "Seeing it in person. I can't believe it."

"We do," said Brad. "Now, you mentioned dollar amounts."

Fleming chuckled awkwardly. "Of course, of course." He swallowed. "May I hold it? Inspect it myself." Another moment of silence fell. Fleming's eyes finally left the book. "I promise, I won't run off with it. With something like this—before I make any kind of offer, I need to be sure."

That made sense to Annie, and Brad hesitated another few moments, before slowly handing the book over to Fleming. Fleming took it, and his fingers trembled softly as he grabbed the book with a gentle touch.

His smile faded, but the excitement in his eyes remained. He rubbed the cover, feeling the texture. He softly squeezed the paper, flipping it over and scrutinizing the back. His fingers ran over the spine, and then over the edge of the pages.

But he didn't open it.

"Do you know the story of JP Harmon?" asked Fleming, as he stared at it.

"Can't say that we do," said Brad.

"Harmon was the pen name for Mike Sullivan, a writer who exclusively published under pen names, because of the blue collar nature of his name. Sullivan wanted to publish his own novels, adult genre novels, but he never got traction with them."

"Where did you see this?"

"If you dig deep enough, you can find interviews with him," said Fleming. "Especially early in his career. He published a sci-fi novel under the name Jack Enfield. It sold poorly, and he struggled to find any more publishing work. But Sullivan wanted to write, and wanted to make a living as a writer. So he worked in kid's genre fiction, and found success writing choose your own adventure novels, first under the popular imprint and then starting his own with Choose Your Fate."

Fleming smiled. "And everything after that—well, a lot of its hearsay. Cobbled together from stories on message boards, and interviews with family members. Sullivan did no interviews after the Choose Your Fate books were published." Fleming squeezed the book in his palm.

"Can I—can I have that back, please?" asked Brad.

Fleming looked up at Brad again and paused, before returning it. "Oh, of course," he said.

Brad took it, and slid it back on the counter, on the other side of him, between him and Annie.

"Did he not like the Choose Your Fate books?" asked Annie.

"Not at first," said Fleming. "He considered the choose your own adventure work beneath him. He went at the work like he was a plumber. And I understand, everyone has to pay their bills. But at some point, it changed."

"What changed?" asked Annie.

"I don't know," said Fleming, looking at her. "It's hard

to say, with so little to go on. But if I had to guess, I think the success emboldened him a little. It made him feel good, made him feel wanted. Something he was writing was working. Even if it was for grade schoolers. And I've read all his work, even all the choose your own adventure books, and there is a turning point, where the books start challenging conventions. The writing gets better, and Sullivan clearly is working in dramatic and important choices for the reader. And that continued until his death."

"Wasn't he killed?" asked Annie.

"That's the story," said Fleming. "But there're all kinds of rumors surrounding it. Saying his wife did it. Or his kids. Or an obsessed fan. But there was no evidence to suggest any of those things. No fingerprints, no murder weapon, no motive."

"Then what happened?" asked Brad.

"No one knows," said Fleming. "But some say that the secret might lie inside that book. The only of its kind, printed as a test before his death, ordered as a proof by Sullivan himself."

"Why would it be in the book?" asked Annie.

"These are just rumors," said Fleming. "All sprung up trying to find an explanation. But it certainly makes the book attractive. I've coveted it for quite a while. I'll pay you twenty thousand dollars for it."

Annie's heart leaped into her throat at the mention of the number. Twenty thousand dollars. It would pay rent for years and give them a safety net. She wanted to yell *yes, yes, sold, sold!* But she held her tongue. Brad betrayed nothing, his poker face holding strong.

"Twenty thousand?" asked Brad. "Is that as high as you'll

go?"

Fleming's smirk had returned, but his eyes betrayed his surprise.

He thought we'd accept it right away.

"Not enough?" asked Fleming.

"We're still entertaining offers," said Brad. "So no, it's not enough."

Fleming's eyes betrayed him again, as well as his nose. Until this point, Annie had only seen excitement and happiness in his face. But now, she saw something else. Anger.

"Thirty," said Fleming. Annie's heart pounded in her chest. The thought of haggling and negotiation made her stomach hurt, and the thought of being handed thirty thousand dollars, just like that, for a book they'd bought the day before for a few hundred made her want to scream with joy.

But Brad didn't budge. He stared back at Fleming.

"Seventy-five, and you can have it," said Brad. Annie pursed her lips to keep herself quiet. She forced herself to breathe. Brad's face stayed impassive, she didn't know how, she felt sweat on her hands—

"Seventy-five?" asked Fleming, his voice raising with incredulity. "You paid one hundred dollars for that lot yesterday. It was supposed to be—" But he cut himself off, and looked away from Brad. Brad didn't budge.

"I'm confident we could make more on the open market, but if you'd like to ensure that you get it today, seventy-five will be what it takes."

"I'll give you fifty," said Fleming, turning back toward Brad, all hint of his smirk gone. His cheeks were turning red. The affability on display since he'd come into the shop was gone.

"The price is seventy-five," said Brad. "It's firm. Considering how much we could fetch at auction, I think it's reasonable."

"Reasonable?!?" asked Fleming, his voice raising.

The money wasn't a problem, until he was asked to pay more.

Brad didn't answer then, only watching Fleming fume. Fleming turned back away from them, and he took several deep breaths. His hands went to his pockets and then turned back.

"Fine," he said, and Annie's heart leaped, thinking he was reaching for his checkbook, but then he turned, and pulled out something and sprayed it at Brad's face, and then hers—

Pepper spray, he had pepper spray

She couldn't see, couldn't breathe, her lungs spasming, and her hands went to her eyes, it hurt so much, so much, and she reached for the book, desperately grasping for it on the counter, and her hands grazed the cover, but then it was pulled from her, and she heard his footsteps and the bell on the door ring, and Fleming was gone with the book.

6

Those idiots.

They let him hold it, left it within reach. A one of one. Literally one of a kind, and they had no security. No cameras, nothing.

Why would he pay for something he could get for free? He didn't make his money by spending all of it.

Andrew walked through his mansion, holding the book in his hand. He had driven home with an eye on his rear-view mirror, but he had calculated correctly. He didn't think they'd follow him. Not after the pepper spray. By the time they would clear their eyes, and get to a vehicle, he'd be miles away, and once he was on the highway, there was no way they'd catch up, not when he was in the Lambo.

He stayed over one hundred MPH on the interstate for

an hour. They would never catch up.

And even better, no proof he stole it. As far as everyone else knew, this was in his lot, that he paid good money for. He had done the right thing and paid top dollar for the damn rare books. He wanted this book, and he had paid for it once, and he would not pay for it twice.

Those damn hicks. Thinking they'd get another 75K from him. He had offered fifty! Fifty grand. That's what they get for being greedy.

He stared at the book and smiled. He loved just holding it. Just possessing it, this incredibly rare thing, felt like ecstasy.

Nothing in the world could match that feeling. He'd done every drug known to man, eaten the most exotic foods, fucked every kind of woman he could find, and traveled at the fastest speeds technology would allow.

All of them were fun for a time, but nothing rivaled owning something unique, possessing the rarest things the world could provide.

Andrew passed into the collections room, a room he'd had built for this explicit, specific purpose. He wanted to display all his things, everything within view.

But it wasn't for guests. He knew other rich people, people who wanted to show off their wealth. They'd have priceless paintings in their living room, and be sure to give you a tour through the grounds of their estate, so you could see the rare cars they had, and the racehorses, and the—

It bored him.

Andrew rarely had visitors. He didn't want to show off his wealth, or his collection. This wasn't for others. It was for *him*.

No, this room was so he could be close to all of his things, all of his collections. So he could bask in their presence.

The room was massive, the outer walls all display cases, segmented off into various smaller units. He'd spent a fortune to make the cases modular, so that he could move and display things exactly how he wanted, to his heart's content.

It was sports cards at first, but as the prices rose, Andrew's enjoyment fell, and he went after comic books, and then toys, and finally books. He would chase each interest for a while, and then the pleasure would die, just like with the drugs, and women, and adrenaline.

But that's what he loved about collecting, is that there were always more things to collect, another niche, another hobby that he could dip into, and find the rarities, and take them, and *keep* them. There was never an end, no bottom to the well. If he started getting bored, he could start a new collection, of antiques, of pottery, of paintings.

Andrew sat down in the leather armchair in the center of the room, an array of singular display cases surrounding him, each highlighting his most prized possessions, the pieces of the collection he liked to look at most. They were currently a near mint Mickey Mantle baseball card, an early Batman appearance comic, and a first printing of The Hobbit he'd gotten at a good price. There was an empty display case, though, one he had emptied for this book in particular.

The Mystery of the Sentinel Lodge would have its home, its home until he rotated it out into one of the cases in the wall. But it would live there forever, be his until he died.

But even then, his possessions would never go to someone else. He had plans, even after his death, for a museum to be built, with his name, for all his collections to be shown far into the future. Well after his death, his collection would still be *his.*

Andrew stared at the book, smiling without even realizing it. His fingers felt the old paper. It was in terrific condition for its age, especially for something not graded or sealed in plastic. He would get that done as well, to ensure its value forever. Sure, no one would ever read it again, but who cared? Keeping it safe and secure was far more important.

But not yet. First, he would read it. And he'd be the last, aside from the grader themselves.

He went to open it, and then he paused.

Could the stories be true?

Those two rubes at the bookstore ate up his story about Sullivan, about him embracing writing choose your own adventure books. Truth was, Sullivan was a miserable bastard who hated writing genre books, and despised writing choose your own adventure books even more. From all accounts, Sullivan even loathed he was good at it, despite the fact it made him all his money. Eh, it worked as a distraction and lulled those two into a false sense of security.

Andrew hadn't told them the truth about Sullivan, and hadn't mentioned the stories he'd heard about the book, from his close contacts in the book collecting world.

He'd learned of the existence of it, and immediately, he wanted it. And when he heard the stories—he'd wanted it even more.

Not because he believed them, of course not, he wasn't a child. No, he wanted the book because of the *mystique.* Because of the story. Because of its rarity.

Why did you collect anything?

Because it was special.

And what was more special than a book that had killed its author?

At least, that was the story Andrew had heard. Sullivan had died, with multiple deep lacerations. No suspects, no evidence, and no motives.

But the legend went that he was holding this book when he died. That the book itself killed Sullivan, and had gone on to kill more.

And not even that—that if you finished the book, finished the adventure, and made the right choices, it would reward you—reward you with—

That's a bunch of bullshit, and you know it.

Andrew didn't believe any of it. Why would he? He wasn't a kid. He believed in the real world, and in dollars and cents. Sullivan was a bastard, who'd gotten the wrong person mad, and they had killed him. And did a good job of cleaning up after their crime.

For any subsequent deaths?

People died all the time. And it's not like anyone had a history of who owned the book. Most people probably sold it because they needed the money.

As for the reward? Even more ridiculous. Pure fantasy.

Pure fantasy.

But there was a part of him, deep inside, that was curious. And he was going to read the book, anyway, right? Might as well try to find the real ending, the true ending. Follow the right path, and get the reward. Even if it's not real, he'll know. He'll be the only one with the knowledge of what lay at the end of the book.

A piece of the collection even more valuable than the

book itself. And after he read it, and got it graded and sealed in plastic, it'd ensure that he'd be the last to ever know.

All he had to do was read the book. He had paused, now he was delaying, he knew he was. A sharp point of dread festered in his guts, and—

What are you afraid of? The book? Don't be silly, Andrew.

He held the slim book in his hands. He'd never been much of a reader, but he'd read a few of these as a kid. It probably wasn't any different from those—

There's only one of these.

Andrew smiled at the thought, and flipped it open, and started reading.

Your breath catches in your lungs as the chill air enters them. You stand outside of the Sentinel Lodge, six stories tall, staring down at you. The Rockies surround you, mountains towering high.

A voice startles you.

"You must be my new assistant caretaker," said the voice, and you turn to see a man who looks to be in his 50s, with graying hair and cold eyes. They are squinted against the glare of the sun off the snowpack.

"I am," you say.

"I'm Carl Douglas," he says, and he extends a hand. You reach out and shake it, his hand big, enveloping yours, and he smiles as he squeezes.

"Nice to meet you," he said. "Follow me inside."

TURN TO PAGE 3

Andrew read, flipping to page 3.

"It's a beautiful hotel, is it not?" asked Carl, as you enter the wooden double doors. You look up to see the elevated ceilings in the lobby, with off-white walls decorated with ornate art, spanning multiple decades and even centuries. Intricate chandeliers hang above you, and for a split-second, you imagine one crashing down on top of you, its many pieces of glass cutting you into a million pieces—

"All original art," said Carl, interrupting your thoughts. Light penetrated through high windows, illuminating the lobby.

Carl continues to show you around, first the lobby, then the maintenance areas, and finally to the grand garden outside, with a massive hedge maze adjacent.

"Take a good look," he says. "We're getting a huge snowfall. After tonight, all of this will be buried."

Andrew read. Carl led him to his room, to relax, warning him not to leave his room during the night. The sun sets, and it snows, and Andrew was given the choice to stay in his room, or to venture out.

"Which path to choose?" asked Andrew, muttering to himself. His eyes were focused on the book, and only on thc book, and he didn't notice the room around him slowly change.

He left his room, because it wouldn't be an adventure if he didn't leave his room, and it wouldn't get his character anywhere if he stayed cooped up all night.

You prowl the halls of the Sentinel Lodge. Suddenly, you hear the sound of a voice. No, not one voice, but two. The voices of two children, and you look down the hallway to see them, in matching blue outfits, staring.

"Please," they say. "Please play with us."

You reach out your hand, as if to help, but they're a hundred feet away, and then they turn, and walk up the stairs. You start to go after them, when you hear a thumping, a heavy thudding noise from below you, on the ground floor.

TO GO UPSTAIRS, TURN TO PAGE 23

TO GO DOWNSTAIRS, TURN TO PAGE 61

"What the hell do I do?" asked Andrew, muttering to himself. The room shifted around him, the glass display cases shifting into wood paneling. The floor beneath him changing into patterned carpeting.

The kids are a trap. Go downstairs.

"But maybe they're not," he whispered. "Maybe I need to play with them to win."

Save your place, and come back if it's a false road.

Andrew slid a thumb to save the page, and flipped to page 61.

You turn away from the twins and walk downstairs, pursuing the mysterious thumping noise. Whatever it is, it needed to be fixed. You are the assistant caretaker, and you will take care of it.

The thumping gets louder and louder as you go down the stairs, and follow the noise into the kitchen. The noise is incredibly loud now, and you realize it's not a thumping noise, but instead, a chopping noise. It's the sound of butchering.

You then see the source of the sound, right in the middle of the kitchen. It's Carl, his back to you. He raises an axe, high into the air above his head, and brings it down with a terrible

CCHUNNK. Your foot catches a metal table with a clang, and he stops, and turns.

His eyes are red and full of menace, and you can see past him now, and there's a body in the middle of the kitchen floor, a torso, broken into pieces, ribs and organs and meat and blood splattered all over the floor. Carl himself is covered in it, with a smattering of blood around his mouth.

He's been sampling as he goes.

He stares at you, and smiles a maniacal smile, and grips the axe with two hands.

"I told you to stay in your room," says Carl, and lunges at you.

The feeling of an axe cracking your skull is the last thing you feel.

Your decision to come downstairs spells your doom, and seals your fate.

THE END

"No, no, no," said Andrew. "Goddamnit, I just started." Luckily, he had saved his spot, his thumb saving where he had chosen wrong, and he flipped back to that page.

He saw it only for a second, however, as the book snapped shut on his thumb.

What the fuck? thought Andrew, but only for moment, because the book hadn't snapped shut on his thumb, but *through* his thumb. He raised his hand, and his thumb was gone, severed neatly, and blood weakly squirted out of the hole where his thumb used to be.

"What the fuck?!?" yelled Andrew, and then he looked up, and around. "Where the fuck—"

"I told you to stay in your room," growled a voice from

down the hall, the hall that shouldn't be there, and Andrew looked down, and his hardwood floor was gone, replaced by a patterned carpet. He turned toward the voice, and he was in the Sentinel Lodge, and Carl stalked down the hallway, blood splattered, holding an axe in two hands.

None of this made sense, the book wasn't real, the book *wasn't real,* and Andrew turned and ran, his reality gone, replaced by the Sentinel Lodge and its murderous caretaker. He was in a hallway, one of the many long hallways of the hotel, and he tried a door, and then another, and they were all locked.

"We follow *THE RULES* at the Sentinel Lodge," growled Carl, gaining ground on him, loping after him, at an uneven gait. His eyes shone in the dim light of the hallway, and Andrew turned and ran upstairs.

The twins were upstairs, he could find them, and make his way out.

But he went up one flight, and turned, running down the hallway, and he saw them, and they stood and stared, and he blinked, and they were gone, replaced by a horrible specter of a woman, ethereal blue, with distorted features, contorted, wailing, and she screamed, and he turned away and Carl was right there.

Carl brought down the axe straight into Andrew's chest, and his breath was gone, and blood poured from the wound in his torso.

Carl stood above him.

"We follow the rules here," he said with a wild smile, and brought the axe down onto Andrew's face.

7

"What do we do?"

Brad sighed. It was the next day, first thing in the morning. Annie's eyes still stung, even after washing them out a dozen times and using therapeutic eye drops from the drugstore. Brad's were red, bloodshot, and she knew hers looked the same.

They hadn't chased after Fleming after he stole the book. By the time they both could see again, he was gone, down the road, with it in hand, and neither her aging SUV or Brad's minivan would catch him.

Instead, they took care of their eyes, and cooled down.

"What do we do?" asked Brad, meeting her stare. "We do nothing, Annie. We eat shit."

Annie exhaled through her nose, and felt something rise

in her chest, a feeling she knew but felt rarely, not in this way.

"We can't—"

"What can we do?" asked Brad. "Fleming is rich. I got in touch with some contacts. They know him, know him well. He hit it big with an app early on, sold out, and retired to a life of collecting. He could buy us a dozen times over."

"I don't give a shit how rich he is," said Annie, venom snaking into her words.

"It's only a part of it," said Brad. "We have no proof that we ever owned that book."

"It was in *our* lot—"

"And zero proof that Fleming took it from us," said Brad. "We don't have security cameras—"

"I'm not going to contribute to whatever the hell police state—"

"I'm not saying I disagree with you, Annie," said Brad, his voice level. "But facts are facts. If we went to the police, nothing would happen. There's no proof of anything, and if we pursued a court case, he can afford a better lawyer, for longer, than we can."

Annie's breath felt hot in her lungs, and she breathed it out, burning past her throat and teeth. She felt anger. She felt rage, a feeling that rarely bubbled up inside her. She believed in the best of people, she believed in extending grace, but this man had come into their small store, assaulted them, and stole their lifeline.

There was another feeling there, buried inside the anger and the rage. What was it?

Deja vu.

There was a strange feeling that she'd done this before.

But that didn't make any sense. None at all, especially because this desperate burning desire to steal the book back wasn't like her at all—

Annie dismissed it. They needed to get the book.

"I don't care," said Annie, finally.

"What?"

"I want our book back," said Annie. "It's not his. He stole it from us."

"I just said—"

"I don't care, Brad," said Annie. "You said you talked to your contacts? They know Fleming?"

"Yes," said Brad. "He's very active, not just in book collecting, but in several different collecting circles. Most of my contacts have done business with him. None of them like him."

"But they know him? They know where he lives?"

"Well, yes," said Brad. "I don't see how that helps—"

"We track him down. We go to his house, and we get our book back."

"Annie—"

"It's *our* book, Brad," said Annie. "And I don't care if we have any proof. I'm not sitting back and letting him take this from us."

"What do you think is going to happen if we go there? You think he'll just answer the doorbell and engage in a nice, normal conversation?"

Annie stared at him, smoke coming from her nostrils.

"I am not suggesting we go talk to him, Brad. I am suggesting we get our book back."

"How?"

"We take it," said Annie. "By hook or by crook."

Brad's face changed from weariness to doubt, his eyebrows raising into a question mark.

"Annie, have you ever stolen anything in your life?"

"Of course I have."

"On purpose?"

"Well—no," said Annie, finally cracking a small smile, the heat dissipating.

"How are *we* going to steal our book back?"

"I don't know," said Annie, looking away. "But we can't do nothing. It's not right."

"He's not going to just let us have it."

"No," said Annie. "But I have a plan."

*

"You don't have a plan," said Brad, as they pulled up to Fleming's house, a gigantic mansion in the suburbs of Boston. It sat on a mammoth lot, with a couple cars sitting in the driveway. The house stood three stories tall, white, with mid-century design.

"Sure, I do," said Annie.

"We can't just knock on the door," said Brad. "He won't answer, and he'll just be more wary if we try again. And he assuredly has a doorbell camera, or something similar."

"Yeah, probably."

"We'll be on camera," said Brad. "If he calls the police, it'll look like *we* are stealing from *him*."

"We disable the cameras."

"How do we do that?" asked Brad. "Neither of us is a hacker."

Annie reached into the glove box of her car and pulled

the wirecutters she had grabbed from home. "We don't have to hack anything," she said. "We have these. And all those cameras rely on an internet connection."

"And?"

"And I looked at Streetview before we left," said Annie. "It's a relatively recent picture—" she keened her neck, and looked behind them, to near the street. "Yep, still there. That's his internet box. We crack it open, and cut the wires. No internet, no cameras, no record of us being here."

"Someone will see us."

"Yeah, probably," said Annie. "That's why I brought these." She reached behind the seat and handed Brad a reflective vest. "Wear this."

"What are we, cable guys?"

"Exactly," said Annie, and then got out of the car, with Brad scrambling behind her.

It had been two days since Fleming had come into their store, pepper sprayed them, and ran off with their book, but the rage was fresh, and it still drove Annie. She knew it wasn't healthy. Frankly, it was stupid, but she didn't care. She walked to the box and popped it open. Only a few cables laid inside, and she snipped through them all, just to be sure. Brad had caught up to her, just in time to see her cut the cables.

"We're going to get arrested."

"No, we're not," said Annie. "Now, you're going to go up to the door and knock on it."

"Why am I going to do that?"

"Because I'm going to sneak around the side and find a way in," said Annie. "And while you're distracting Fleming, I'm going to find the book."

"What? Wait—"

But Annie didn't wait for Brad to disagree. She had never done anything like this before, and she never would, not normally, but she was right, she knew she was right, filled with righteous anger, and it would carry her far. She walked to the side of the property, hugging a fence. The street was quiet, and Annie walked with purpose but didn't run, getting to a wooden gate that had no lock, and she opened it, and was in the backyard. She caught a final glimpse of Brad, who walked to the front door, and then the gate slammed shut behind her and she was alone.

She walked alongside the house, testing every window as she passed. All of them were locked tight. She heard no alarms from inside the house. If she had to, she'd break glass, but she wouldn't have to, there had to be one open, everyone forgot to lock something.

She came to the backyard, and it was huge, with a gigantic swimming pool and matching hot tub. Both were covered for the winter, with a giant shade canopy draped above them.

A sprawling patio led to it, and Annie climbed up, facing towering windows and double French doors. The windows were locked. The doors were assuredly locked as well—right?

Annie went to the French doors, only darkness inside, the dim winter sunlight only reaching so far. She tried the handles, and one turned, and she cautiously pulled it open.

No alarm rang, and she waited, and listened, and there were no footsteps from inside, rushing to confront her. Only silence.

She pulled the door open and slipped inside, closing

it behind her. All the lights were off, only the sun lighting what appeared to be a room set aside for entertaining, with a bar on the side, a piano, and some small bar top tables, surrounded by stools.

But the room was sparsely decorated, and as she pushed into the rest of the house, it wasn't an outlier. The house had little furniture. The living room had a large leather couch, but nothing else, and the walls were empty. It felt like a showcase model for a home builder, not a house someone lived in.

Focus, Annie.

She moved through the house, listening for Fleming, but hearing nothing. There was no sign of him, or of Brad, for that matter. She thought she would hear him knocking on the door, but there was nothing.

She crept through Fleming's home, seeing no signs of life.

Creeeeeak.

The noise of a floorboard shifting reached her, and Annie instinctively ducked against a wall. It came from her right, and she waited, and listened again. Muffled footsteps, softly moving.

Annie peeked around the corner, toward the noise, and saw some light, through a dark room, and found the source of the sound.

It wasn't Fleming.

It was Brad.

What the hell? How did he get in?

Annie sneaked toward Brad, through the darkened room, toward the light. Brad stood in the center of the next room, looking down.

What was he doing?

She walked forward, light on her toes, and entered the room, opposite Brad, but then was caught off guard. The walls were all glass, segmented off, ornate and special in a way nothing else in the house was. The glass displays contained Fleming's collection, she saw, and her eyes caught comic books, and baseball cards, and books. Her eyes stuck on a first edition of The Hobbit. She had seen it before in rare book shops, and online, and had always coveted it. But it had always been expensive, far too pricey for her to stomach. And there it sat, among other items she knew were rare as well.

The room was full of them. She was agog at all of them, the power of the items distracting her from the mission at hand. She realized she was distracted, and her eyes danced between the items now, looking for their book, for the hollow eyes of the eerie twins staring out at the reader.

But no. It wasn't there.

"Annie," said Brad. She looked at him, finally, his eyes meeting hers. Annie then noticed the stench. It smelled rank in here.

"What are you doing in here, Brad?"

"The front door was open," said Brad. "So I came in."

"Shh," said Annie. "We don't know where he is."

"Annie," said Brad. "Open your eyes." He gestured down to the floor at his feet. A chair stood in front of them, and Annie couldn't see around it. She moved to the left, and she saw what Brad motioned toward. It was Fleming.

"Fuck!" yelled Annie.

"He's dead."

"Yeah, I know!" said Annie, backing away, looking off.

She had never seen a dead body before, Jesus Christ, she hadn't expected—

"Come look at this."

"I don't want to—"

"Someone killed him," said Brad. Annie turned, despite herself, and looked. Fleming's head was cleaved in two, and blood and brains covered the floor, and she looked away again, swallowing down her breakfast, which threatened to come back up.

"Brad, I can't—"

"He's holding our book," said Brad. Annie turned, and avoided looking at the carnage, instead looking at his hand, outstretched, the *Choose Your Fate* book clutched in it.

"We have to call the police," said Annie.

"And tell them what?"

"That we found Fleming this way," said Annie. "We clearly didn't kill him. From the smell, he's been dead a while. Brad? What are you doing?"

Brad knelt next to the body, one hand pulling his shirt over his nose. He touched their book, snaking fingers around it, without touching Fleming. He tugged it away from Fleming's death grip, pulling it once, twice, and then free. Brad stood up with the book, and then tucked it away. He stared at Annie.

"We can call the police now," he said.

*

The police believed them.

They had said they had come to do business with Fleming about books. If they dug deeper, nothing they said would be proven untrue. They only lied a little, and the police had no reason to doubt them.

They didn't mention *The Mystery of the Sentinel Lodge*, nor Fleming visiting them two days prior.

They drove back, the stereo playing quietly, the heat keeping out the approaching winter cold. Annie held the book in her hands, staring at it.

"It was ours," said Brad. "If we mentioned any of it, we might never get it back."

Annie said nothing in return. Brad was right, he was. They had only gone there to get their book back, and now they had it again, free to sell it, a winning lottery ticket that was rightfully theirs.

She stared at the book, held in her hands, as Brad drove. Clean and neat, looking as mint as when she had first found it, among the books in their lots. No sign of where it had been, or what it had weathered.

But Annie knew it had seen two deaths. Had been the last thing two people had read, ever.

A question lingered in her mind.

Was it only two?

Or was it more?

8

"Are we not going to talk about it?"

Annie scanned in books, while Brad tidied up the store shelves, his laptop open near her behind the counter. Only they occupied the store, although it had gotten busy a few times. Annie was thankful.

Anything to take her mind off the terrible death of Fleming, and the horrible carnage that still passed in front of her eyes when she closed them.

But now they were alone, and Fleming's death clung to the inside of her mind in the quiet.

"Talk about what?" asked Brad, sorting books in the mystery section.

"About Fleming."

"What is there to talk about?" asked Brad. "We got the

book back. The police believed us. I doubt they'll contact us again. Free and clear. Not that we really did anything wrong."

"You saw him, you saw—what was left of his face."

"Yeah," said Brad. He squeezed his eyes shut briefly, and then re-opened them, and stopped sorting them. "It was rough. But it's over. He sure as hell isn't going to get the book back now."

Annie exhaled. "How can you say something like that?"

"I'm sorry," said Brad. "But I can't feel sorry for him. What did he do?"

"He stole our book."

"Exactly," said Brad. "He fucking pepper sprayed us, and stole our book, that we bought, fair and square."

"He's dead, Brad—"

"And? You want to know something, Annie? When I asked around about him, with all my contacts, they all disliked him. More than that, some people absolutely hated him. The few who still did business with him only did it because he was rich, and they needed the money. He was a royal asshole, and now he's dead. The world is better off with some people dead, and Fleming is one of them."

"It's more than that," said Annie, looking down, closing her eyes. She saw his massacred face. She opened them again. "He was holding the book."

"Well, it made it easy for us to find."

"That's not what I mean," said Annie. "That's two, Brad. Two people who were holding the book when they died." She looked at Brad again, and he looked back, confused.

"Wait—do you think the book itself has something to do with this?"

Annie paused. "It—it doesn't feel right. Something's wrong with it."

"It's just a book, Annie. A valuable one, sure, but it's not magic. It's just rare. I'm sure if you trace the ownership of a lot of rare, valuable things, you'll see a lot of hardship and tragedy along the way, just because desperate and obsessed people are drawn toward this stuff."

"Desperate?" asked Annie. "Do we count as desperate?"

"I would say so," said Brad. "Especially with something like that book."

"I don't like it."

"You were the one who wanted to go back and get it."

"Yeah, when there wasn't another death attached to it," said Annie. "How many more have died, that we don't know about?"

"Look around, Annie," said Brad. "A lot of our books were last touched by now dead people. It's how we've gotten a lot of our stock. It's not a bad thing, and it doesn't mean these books are cursed, or whatever."

"This wasn't natural causes," said Annie. "His face—" Annie paused.

Brad put the mystery books back, and came over to Annie. "The first time we met Fleming, properly, he pepper sprayed us, and stole from us. It took him less than ten minutes to make us enemies. And all we are is booksellers. Relatively kind and non-violent people. But I guarantee that none of that entered his mind. To Fleming, anyone he could steal from is someone he *should* steal from. Well, he took something from someone a lot more dangerous than us, and they didn't take kindly to it. I know it was hard to see. I didn't like it myself. But do your best to forget it. It's behind us now. Fleming is dead, and he's the police's problem. We got our book back."

"I don't want it anymore."

"Well, I'm going to do my best to get rid of it," said Brad. "And get us a substantial amount of money in the process."

"It's safe, right?"

"It's locked away at the house," said Brad. "The safe is fireproof, and impregnable to anyone but the most experienced lockpick. I don't expect anyone to come and get it, anyway. You'll never see it again."

Annie met his gaze. Brad *was* trying to reassure her. And he was right.

He was right.

"Fair enough," said Annie. "I'll do my best."

"That's all you can do," said Brad. "Speaking of, I'm going to go home, and make some calls. I sent out feelers about the book, and I'm hoping one of them will bite, without us having to send it to auction. It'll make everything easier."

Brad closed his laptop, grabbed his messenger bag, and headed out the door. Annie stopped him.

"Brad, wait," she said, and he paused at the door.

"Yes?"

"Will you do something for me? I know it's crazy—"

"What is it?"

"Don't read the book," said Annie.

"Annie—"

"I know, I know," she said. "But there's something wrong with it. I know it. Please, for me."

Brad stared for a second longer. "I won't read it. Scout's honor."

"Thank you," said Annie, and Brad went out the door.

*

"So, what did he say? Does he have interest?" asked Brad.

"Are you firm on 100K?" asked Ted, on the phone.

"Yes," said Brad. "This is the only chance you'll have prior to it going to auction."

Brad paced through his house, through the living room, into the kitchen, and turning back around, and going back through the living room, down the hallway, and into their bedroom, and then back again. He never could stay still on a phone call, especially not a business call. His nerves would eat him alive if he wasn't moving, and he needed every ounce of nerve he had. If they could clinch a sale before heading to market—it would solve all their problems.

Well, not all their problems. Brad had talked a big game with Annie, but seeing Fleming's body had bothered him.

But it was worth it to get the book back, and soon, they wouldn't have to worry about it at all, only what to do with their money.

"Can you go down to 75K? He'd be firm at 75," said Ted. Ted was a dealer, an agent, a middleman, that Brad used from time to time to get access to some real high-rollers in the collecting and book world. He came from publishing, and seemed to know everyone. Ted would want a cut, a few grand, but it was worth it for who he knew. And Ted was honest, which was worth a few grand alone.

"Sorry," said Brad. "We're not going under one hundred. This is a one of a kind. Nothing like it on Earth. There never will be another one, and we want to get what it's worth."

There was silence on the other end, and Brad let Ted have it. He was thinking.

"Fine," said Ted. "He'll do it, then."

"What? Really?"

"Yes," said Ted. "He gave me the go ahead. You're right, it's one of a kind. It's obviously contingent on condition and contents, but I trust you, Brad, so I expect everything to be kosher."

"Of course, of course. I'll drive it to you. When? Tomorrow work?"

"Can't do tomorrow," said Ted. "I'm free on Wednesday. Meet me for lunch. We'll go someplace nice."

They hashed out the details, but Brad did so with a smile on his face. They said goodbye and Brad fist pumped hard, jogging around his house, beaming.

They did it.

After the nightmare that was getting the book back from Fleming, now they had it, and they had secured their payday. 100 grand. Talking about it was one thing, but confirming it was another, and Ted was true to his word. If he thought the book was kosher, he'd have the money to Brad in no time at all. And sure, maybe they could get more for it at auction, but that wasn't guaranteed, and the longer they held onto the book, the higher the chances that more shady shit would happen. Another Andrew Fleming might come around, and take it from them. Better to cash out now, and use that money to make the store bigger and better. Or just to give them a little more security.

He thought to call Annie, to tell her the good news. She'd be overjoyed, and maybe the sale would help banish the ominous mood that had settled over her since they'd returned from Fleming's house.

Not that he blamed her.

He had put on a brave face, but he didn't enjoy seeing

Fleming in that state any more than she did. He had worked as a paramedic during college, and seen far worse than that, but still, you never got used to it. If you thought you had—you needed help, and quick.

But they *hadn't* killed Fleming, and they *had* gotten their book back, and sure Annie had been upset, but the news would buoy her spirits. He knew it would. Less to worry about, with that amount in the bank.

But he wouldn't call her yet. No, he had something to do first.

Brad went upstairs, to his and Gabby's bedroom, and opened the closet, and pulled up a cabinet door. Inside was their safe, and he typed in the six-digit code, and it beeped open.

The safe wasn't anything fancy, but it would do the job for anyone but an expert, and he pulled out the book that had sat inside since they'd returned from Fleming's.

On Wednesday, it would go to Ted, and Brad would get a hundred grand. But there was something he needed to do first.

You promised her.

Yeah, he had. He had promised Annie he wouldn't read the book. And that was all well and good, but Ted wanted a guarantee on condition and contents, and Brad's word was on the line. If he brought Ted the book, and Ted opened it up in front of him, and inside was the text from *Twilight,* Brad's reputation would be ruined with Ted for the rest of their lives, and probably sullied with everyone that Ted knew, which was most of the bookselling contacts in the Northeast.

Brad wouldn't be able to do anything high-end, ever

again.

So he had to verify the contents of the book.

Was it probably pointless?

Probably. The book was probably exactly what it looked to be.

But he wasn't willing to sacrifice his reputation on that, and not on a promise he made to Annie to ease her mind.

He had to know what was inside the book. And despite how much he loved Annie, and trusted her, she was clearly flustered by their experience at Fleming's house. The book had nothing to do with the two men's deaths. It was a coincidence, and a limited perspective. Nothing more. It wasn't magic, and it wasn't cursed.

Gabby and Buddy were visiting her mother for the week, and Brad had the whole house to himself. He grabbed the book, and returned to the couch. It was perfect weather to lie back, under a blanket, and read through *The Mystery of the Sentinel Lodge.* He would cruise through the book, happy knowing that when he was done, they'd be a hundred thousand dollars richer.

He reclined, throw pillow behind his head, and cracked open the book.

Your breath catches in your lungs as the chill air enters them. You stand outside of the Sentinel Lodge, six stories tall, staring down at you. The Rockies surround you, mountains towering high.

A voice startles you.

"You must be my new assistant caretaker," said the voice, and you turn to see a man who looks to be in his 50s, with graying hair and cold eyes. They are squinted against the glare

of the sun off the snowpack.

"I am," you say.

"I'm Carl Douglas," he says, and he extends a hand. You reach out and shake it, his hand big, enveloping yours, and he smiles as he squeezes.

"Nice to meet you," he said. "Follow me inside."

TURN TO PAGE 3

Brad turned the page.

He was a fast reader, always had been. He got to his first ending within five minutes. Killed by Carl, the insane caretaker.

"Well, I've verified the contents," he murmured to himself. Then he looked up and saw that he was no longer in his house.

9

“What the fuck?” asked Brad, sitting up from where he laid on the couch, what had been his comfy couch in his living room, but now was leather, changing underneath him. It sat in front of a roaring fireplace, with other leather armchairs, a decanter of brandy sitting on the table.

He sat in a lounge, big, and warm, from the huge fire that danced before him.

Where am I?

The thought crossed his mind quickly, and then more thoughts fired through in rapid succession, and he stared down at the book.

The Mystery of the Sentinel Lodge.

He had read only a few pages, as his character met the caretaker Carl, was warned to stay in his room, and then disobeyed, to be slaughtered by Carl in the rec room.

A distant string of shouts reached him, from somewhere else in the lodge.

Fuck fuck fuck.

The Sentinel Lodge. Because that's where he was. Annie had warned him, had told him the book was cursed. He had dismissed her, because of course he had, it was just a book. But even then, there's a difference between people who owned it dying from mysterious circumstances, and the thing *actually killing them*.

This didn't make any goddamn sense. How could this book transport him to the Sentinel Lodge? He tried to open it again, but it was sealed shut, impossible to even get his fingers in.

Denial and doubt wouldn't get him anywhere. He *was* in the Sentinel Lodge. He felt the heat of the fire in front of him. The texture of the leather rubbed against his bare skin. He heard the shouting of Carl, raving somewhere in the lodge. Brad was here, no matter how much sense it didn't make, and ignoring it wouldn't get him out.

He did the math in his head. Eddie had died with no visible wounds. A heart attack? Who knows. Fleming's cause of death was obvious, with the attack to his head. Whatever it was, the book had done it, the Lodge had done it. He heard Carl shout again, this time louder. He was getting closer.

Brad needed to get out of here, someway, somehow.

He was in the lounge, he realized. He had skimmed over the section where Carl had led him on a tour of the grounds, and now he wished he had paid better attention. But the lounge would be on the first floor. He needed to get the hell out of here.

He wore the same clothes he had on when he started reading, so the book didn't transform *him*, as far as he could tell. If there was a snowstorm outside, it would be a cold trek, but he couldn't stay in here.

Brad tucked the book into a pocket and got up. He looked quickly and grabbed a fireplace poker, feeling the weight of the iron in his hand. It felt real, and he swung it once as a test. It was heavy and would cave in a skull with ease. If Carl wanted to come for him, he wouldn't go down easy.

Brad turned and left the lounge, the double doors leading out into a wide hallway that led into a vast lobby. The lights were bright, all the seats empty. A glance out of the large windows revealed only darkness, with an occasional swirl of flying snow floating against the window.

The counter was empty, and he heard thumping noises from above him. Was it Carl? He didn't know, and he didn't want to find out. He'd get the hell out of here. Would leaving the lodge get him back to his world?

Was there anything out there at all?

The lobby was empty, but well-lit, and Brad marched through it, clutching the fireplace poker. Only double wooden doors stood in his way to the outside. He pulled at the heavy doors, but they didn't budge. He pulled again, but they were locked tight.

He wasn't going to be busting through those doors, but massive windows flanked them, and the poker would break through easily. Was it smart to break the windows and let in the cold? He didn't know, but he wanted out, away from whatever the hell this lodge was.

Brad approached the window and reared back to swing—

"I wouldn't do that, son," growled a voice from behind him. Brad reversed, coming face to face with who he guessed was Carl, the caretaker. He was sweaty and grimy, his eyes wild, his hair disheveled. He dragged a fire axe behind him, its blade red from blood. "Don't want to let out the bought air."

Brad held out the poker. "Stay back."

Carl's eyes never left Brad's, staring into his soul, even as the poker waved in front of him.

"Got to be careful with that, son," said Carl. "You might hurt somebody. First lesson of the day. Be careful with your tools."

Brad's eyes went to the axe, still dragging on the ground. The thoughts whipped through his head. Was Carl a normal man, bound to normal physics? Or as a character in this book, was he bound only to the imagination of the reader?

"I want out of here," said Brad. "I want to go home."

"There's no leaving, son," said Carl. "Look outside. Snowstorm will be piling on us for days. Might as well make peace with that."

"Leave me alone," said Brad. "I will use this."

Carl smiled, revealing stained teeth. "Oh, I bet you would. I told you not to leave your room, son. I told you. I'm not responsible for what happens next—"

Brad saw the axe shift then, the blade pivot, and turn, and Carl was lifting it, his other hand shifting to swing it down with two hands, to crack Brad's skull in half like Carl had with Fleming, to leave his corpse for Gabby to stumble upon, his head split in two.

I'm not dying here.

Brad stepped forward, swinging the poker as hard as he could at Carl's head, just as Carl reached back for the axe. Brad was six feet tall and weighed nearly two hundred pounds. He wasn't the strongest man in the world, but he had wrestled in high school and had worked out to keep that muscle for most of his adult life. The poker moved with surprising speed and force, and the curved, sharpened point on the back of the poker broke through Carl's ear and then skull with a sickening THUNK.

Carl immediately went limp and fell to the floor, his hollow, wild eyes still staring straight ahead.

"Fuck," said Brad. His heart thumped in his chest, the surge of adrenaline coursing through him, but the encounter was over before it began. Carl laid still, dead as a doornail. Brad knew he wasn't real. He was only a fictional character.

At least that's what he told himself as he pulled at the poker, trying to reclaim his weapon. Black blood spilled out of the hole in Carl's head as Brad wrenched his weapon loose.

Back to the window. He was getting out of here.

He raised the poker and jammed it into the window.

He expected a crash and the sound of breaking glass.

Instead, he got a soft *thunk*, and the poker bounced off.

What?

Brad rammed the poker into the window again, but nothing happened, just a soft *thunk*, the poker bouncing off like it had hit a rubbery, plastic bubble.

The book won't let you leave.

He was trapped in here. There had to be a way out. There had to be.

Brad pulled the book from his pocket, and stared at it. He tried to open it again, but it still was locked shut. It had to have an answer, but he couldn't get into it.

You got an ending, there is no more reading—

Brad stared at the book, looking for an answer. *Choose Your Fate: The Mystery of the Sentinel Lodge.*

The Mystery of the Sentinel Lodge. Mystery. He had to solve the mystery. Solve the mystery, and he could get out.

What was the mystery?

He stared at the cover. The twins. That had to be it. Why else would they be there?

He had to find out about the twins. He looked to Carl's corpse, and then walked toward the stairs. Brad had to find the twins' room, and find out what happened to them. Maybe set them free? He held the poker in his hand, Carl's blood staining the tip. Regardless if this was real or not, he could stop the things in the lodge. He could kill them. He'd get out of here.

He'd get home.

Upstairs, upstairs. The twins were in the lodge proper, and he had to go upstairs. Without Carl prowling around, there was one less worry.

Brad walked up to the second floor, the poker ready. He reached the landing, and stared down the long hallway, doors lining the walls of each side. The garish carpet and its multi-layered pattern jumped out at him, but he tried to focus. The twins. Where were they?

He could go room to room, but opening random doors in an imaginary haunted hotel felt like a bad choice. Brad went up to the third floor, stepping quietly, the bright carpets absorbing his footsteps. Another long, empty corridor. Despite the silence, despite the emptiness, Brad's stomach ached. Something was wrong, but he didn't know what.

Up to the fourth floor. Nothing, still. Only two more floors. If he didn't see anything, he would have to go room to room.

What if there was nothing else? What if this was all this was, and he was trapped here, with nothing but Carl's corpse, and an endless snowy night?

Brad dismissed it. There was a way out. He would go home. Gabby, and Buddy. He wouldn't let them go.

He took a deep breath and walked upstairs. Halfway up, he heard it. The crying.

It was a soft noise, but a sound he recognized. The first time Buddy cried in the night, they had rushed to his crib. He was fine, and Brad had developed a sixth sense over time, a fine skill to recognize when Buddy had bumped into something and cried over the momentary pain, or when his cries were serious. He could tell the difference now, and this cry wasn't Buddy's, but it was the sound of a sad, scared child, who needed help.

He would help them. He'd get out of here. He'd go home.

Brad rounded the stairs and was on the fifth floor, and the crying was louder now, from down the hall. He moved slowly toward the sound, trying to find the source. He passed door after door, the crying getting louder, and louder, piercing into his heart.

Room 512. Brad arrived in front of the door, and it was clear this was where the crying came from. The door was closed. His heart beat hard in his chest, and the sourness in his stomach wouldn't go away. Could it be a trap? He couldn't dismiss the idea. But he could wander the halls forever, and not find anything.

Fortune favors the bold.

Brad opened the door, still gripping the fireplace poker. If it was a trap, he was ready.

The crying was even louder now, with the door open, almost deafening. It was a fairly standard room, with two beds, and a small bathroom. The crying came from the bathroom.

Brad looked in, the sound getting even louder.

He saw them.

It was the twins from the cover of the book. One of them cried, screaming awful tears into his sister's shoulder, the other holding him as he sobbed. They were covered in something. Not blood. It was black. Grease? Oil?

Their blonde hair was saturated, their simple blue outfits stained black from soaking in death.

Brad stared, and then they saw him, and the crying stopped.

Fuck.

The twin who had wept slowly turned to Brad, his face blank, his eyes black. His sister stared with him. Then they smiled in unison, their mouths widening.

"You didn't protect us," said the girl.

"We only wanted to play," said the boy.

"Let's play, father," said the girl.

"Let's play, daddy," said the boy.

"Let's play," they said, in unison.

The children chanted at him, and they stood, holding hands.

But more than that. They rotted in front of him. Their skin shrunk from their bones, their tissue withering.

"What the fuck," said Brad, backing away. They were dead, they were dead—

"Save us," said the voices, and Brad stumbled back, against the hallway wall, and then he ran, stumbling out of the hotel room, and down the hall. They reached for him with their tiny, rotting fingers. They plead to him with broken jaws.

"Protect us," they said again, and he turned to watch them walk toward him, a slow and steady pace. He didn't know what would happen if they touched him, but he wouldn't find out.

They were behind him, and Brad sprinted as hard as he could. He ran for the stairs, and he didn't bother taking them, jumping over the handrail and half wall, landing a floor down.

He stumbled and fell from the drop, but pushed himself to his feet, and then quickly did it again, dropping another floor. His knees screamed in momentary pain, but he needed to gain some distance on them. He was on the third floor, and heard them above him.

"Play with us," they said.

"Protect us," they said.

Brad moved down the stairs. He needed to get back to the first floor, to barricade himself somewhere. He had to regroup, he was in over his head. Taking two stairs at a time, he rounded down the stairwell, past the second floor, down back onto the first floor, and into the lobby.

The shortcuts had bought him a few extra seconds, and his eyes jumped around the lobby, it was still empty, and where was the lounge? He had gotten turned around, had he gone down the same stairs he went up, he wasn't sure—

"Help us," begged the dead children and Brad saw the door to the lounge. They were right on top of him, it didn't make sense. He could barricade the door with the furniture, and buy himself some time.

He rushed in, slamming the door behind him.

Wait—

This wasn't the lounge. There was no fireplace, no couch, but instead a pool table, billiard balls ready to play—

"No time for fun, boy," said a voice, Carl's voice, and an awful, cracking pain struck Brad in the back, and his legs collapsed out from under him.

No—

He fell to the floor and felt Carl pull his axe from him. Warm blood splashed down his back, and he couldn't move his legs—

Carl stood over him, smiling, the dark hole in the side of his head healed, gone.

"I don't go down so easy, son," said Carl. "Can't say the same for you." He smiled, a delirious smile, and brought the axe up over his head, like he was splitting logs.

Brad feebly put his hand up, to ward off the blow. He thought of Gabby. Of Buddy.

"Please—"

"Good boys don't beg," said Carl, and brought down the axe.

10

"I don't know what to do, Annie."

Gabby sat alone in Buddy's room. She sat against the wall, moving Buddy's toys out of the way. The room was dark, the curtains drawn, the sun leaking in. A soft buzz filtered up from downstairs, the guests eating, drinking, their distant chatter reaching them.

The funeral was well attended. Brad was a popular man, who made friends wherever he went, and even more business associates, who had wanted to pay their respects. Gabby had spoken. She had told the story of how they first met. Of how Brad was the best man she'd ever known. How she saw him in Buddy, and how she would always love him. She hadn't cried.

Annie didn't know how. She had cried when Gabby

had called her, and told her the news, had weeped for the days since, the font of tears never-ending, no matter what she did. Her stomach had ached, a deep pit of sorrow that couldn't be filled.

She had wanted to speak at the funeral. Brad was her best friend, her business partner, and had meant everything to her, and she should say those words out loud, not just for him, and not just for the people assembled, or for herself, but to beat back the sorrow, to help defeat the loss and grief.

But there was no way. The thought of walking to the front of the assembled crowd, of trying to put voice to those words crippled her, her legs collapsing, muscles falling weak and useless. She'd never make it to the podium, her words swallowed by tears.

Annie didn't know how Gabby did it, how she found the strength to not just stand there, but to speak out loud without failing a thousand times.

But Annie saw now. Gabby sat in the darkness, her face empty, her eyes black. She had not held back tears during her speech, not out of utter willpower and fortitude, but because her sadness was beyond them. Annie's grief was an unending spring of them—Gabby's misery had swallowed up every tear she had. She was left with a desert. A barren dune filled with nothing but woe.

Annie sat next to her and said nothing.

"What do I do?" asked Gabby. "We had our whole lives ahead of us. We would watch Buddy grow up. He would leave us and start his own life. We would face hardship, but forge a stronger relationship because of it. We would grow old. Retire. Travel. All together. But now—"

She stopped. Gabby took a great, long breath, breathing in deeply, and then forcing it all out, and Annie heard the pain, the terrible trauma that lurked in her heart, and burned her lungs, and seized her guts. That breath did all it could to push those forces back.

"But now," said Gabby. "It's gone. Blown away in the wind. I'm alone. Buddy—he doesn't have a dad—"

Gabby then leaned into Annie, and buried her face in her shoulder, and then the tears let loose, whatever held them at bay, wherever they had been, they came now, and Gabby cried, sobbing into Annie's shoulder. Annie held her, Gabby shaking with sorrow, quietly crying all the tears she had.

Annie said nothing, holding her.

Gabby cried.

Eventually, she stopped.

Gabby pulled a tissue from a pocket, and wiped her eyes, and blew her nose. She finally looked at Annie again, her eyes bleary.

"Who did it, Annie? Who killed Brad?" she asked, her voice quiet. They hadn't talked about it, couldn't talk about it.

"I don't know."

"Was it the same person who killed Fleming?" asked Gabby. "He was killed the same way. They both had the book—"

"I don't know," said Annie. "Is it still—"

"In the safe? Yes," said Gabby. "I put it in there, and haven't touched it since."

Annie took a breath. "I need it."

"Why?"

"It's the reason, Gabby. I don't know why, or how, but it killed Brad. It killed Fleming. It killed Eddie, the man who owned it prior."

"It's a book, Annie. It can't swing a weapon. It can't hurt you—"

"I want to find out why," said Annie. "I need to know. If the answer is a dead-end, so be it. And if anything—if someone is tracking down the owners of the book, and killing them—I'd rather it be me than you. You've suffered enough."

Gabby took another incredible breath and exhaled.

"Either way, I'll get you an answer," said Annie. "I promise."

Gabby held her gaze for a moment longer, reading Annie's face.

"I can't lose you, too, Annie," said Gabby. "We should just destroy it."

"Brad was working on selling it," said Annie. "If we're going to get rid of it, we should at least get something for it."

"I—I don't think I can."

"I can take care of it," said Annie. "I'll be careful."

Gabby broke her gaze. "Here." She pushed herself to her feet, and she helped Annie up, and led her into the bedroom, where she pulled open the closet door. She kneeled, and keyed in the code for the safe that sat within a cabinet, and opened it. The book lay on top.

Gabby stopped, staring at it.

"Gabby?" asked Annie, quietly.

"Take it," said Gabby. "I don't know if I can touch it again." Annie bent down and took it from the top, and clutched it in her hand. It looked the same as when she had pulled it from the pile of books from the estate sale.

Gabby closed the safe, the cabinet, and the closet, everything back the way it was—

Not the way it was, Brad was dead—

"I'm going to go back downstairs," said Annie. "Do you need anything else right now?"

Gabby glanced at her. "I'll be down in a few minutes. Just need some time alone."

Annie nodded, and then went downstairs, grabbing her purse from the banister where she had hung it, and pulling it over her shoulder and tucking the book inside.

The crowd had thinned a little, with some of the guests, having made their appearance, departing. Annie grabbed a drink and headed outside, where there were some tables and chairs set up for any overflow. She took an empty chair at an unattended table and sipped at her fruit punch. She wanted to leave, wanted to go hunt down the true source of this book, and find out if Fleming had lied to them.

Find out who or what killed Brad.

But she wouldn't abandon Gabby. Annie would be the last one to leave, or among them.

"Annie?"

She turned and saw Ted Montour, wearing a dark suit, tinted aviators covering his eyes. She had met him once before, and knew Brad did business with him once in a while. Ted was older, in his late 50s, and clearly had some work done on his face, which was devoid of wrinkles. He extended a hand, and Annie took it. He shook softly.

"I'm sorry for your loss, kid," he said. "May I?"

"Sure," said Annie, gesturing to a chair near her. Ted took it, slowly setting himself down into it.

"He was too young," said Ted. "I had just talked to him."

Annie only nodded. She wasn't good at small talk on a normal day, and on a day like this—

"Speaking of," said Ted. "I don't mean to be rude, Annie, so I hope you'll forgive me for talking business. But Brad and I had negotiated a deal to buy a book you both had acquired—"

Annie's stomach sunk.

"—it was a choose your own adventure book, but only one was ever published. I had a very interested buyer, and we had agreed to a one hundred thousand dollar price point, so you can understand my urgency. If you can deliver the book, I can deliver payment. I'm sure the money could be useful for Brad's wife—"

Annie's heart leapt into her throat. A hundred thousand?

But then she realized, and it all clicked. Gabby had found the book in Brad's hands, just like Fleming. Just like Eddie. He had agreed to sell the book to Ted, and had wanted to read it before the hand-off.

And it had killed him.

The book was tucked in her purse. She could pass it off to Ted, get a life-changing check, and never have to worry about it again. But if it was truly cursed—if it did kill people, someway, somehow—she'd just be dooming the next person to an untimely death, trading it for a hefty amount of blood money.

And also losing her connection to what killed her best friend.

And that overruled everything. While she still had the book, she still had that connection, the key to the source of whatever power it had. Without it, it was gone, and so were any answers.

Take the money, and move on!

Her brain screamed at her. Nothing would bring Brad

back, and his absence only made the payday more important. It could carry her and help Gabby as she adjusted to having only a single income.

But more than anything, she needed to know, needed to know what killed Brad, what entity attacked and murdered him. And without the book, that answer would be even harder to find.

"I have it," said Annie. "But I can't sell it. Not yet."

Ted stared at her, his eyes hidden behind his aviators.

"Can I ask why not?"

Annie chose her words carefully. "Because I think the book may be connected to Brad's death. In fact—" She paused, and looked at Ted. Ted was connected, Brad had mentioned many times.

"Do you know anyone who knew JP Harmon? Or Mike Sullivan, his real name?"

Ted paused, and then removed his sunglasses, revealing dark hazel eyes, eyes older than his face. He considered her, for a moment.

"You think his death is related?"

"Yes," said Annie. She wasn't lying.

Ted softly nodded. "Yeah, I knew Mike. Not well, but well enough. Knew his wife too. I think she's still kicking."

"His wife? His widow?"

"Yeah," said Ted. "I have a number for her, but I don't know if it's any good. I have an address, too. Don't know if that's any good either." He took a breath. "I can give you them. But—"

"But what?"

"I want assurances that you won't sell the book to anyone else."

Annie nodded. “That’s fair enough. If I sell it, Ted, it’ll be to you. I’ll put it in writing, if you want.”

“That’s not necessary,” said Ted. “I could always trust Brad, and I trust you the same.” He pulled out his phone, and scrolled for minutes, until finding what he was looking for. Ted pulled out the small memorial program, and jotted down a phone number and address, and labeled it *Judy Sullivan*. He handed it over to Annie.

“It’s in Pennsylvania, a distant suburb of Pittsburgh.”

“Not very close,” said Annie.

“A day’s drive,” said Ted. “Could be worse. Wait a second. Can I have that back?”

Annie handed it back over, and Ted scrawled something else down. Another phone number.

“That’s my number,” said Ted. “Let me know, one way or the other.”

“I will,” said Annie. “Thank you, for helping, and understanding.”

“We weren’t close or anything, but everyone deserves an answer. And no one deserves to die like that. Good luck.” And then he stood up and was gone, walking back to his car.

11

The phone number was disconnected, and the address's property records showed it owned by someone who wasn't Judy Sullivan. Annie pored through internet searches for hours, trying to find any report of Judy in Jefferson Township, the distant suburb of Pittsburgh the address was located in. Nothing in Pittsburgh either.

Annie knew Mike Sullivan was dead, and knew that Judy Sullivan was still alive as of a few years ago. But beyond that, the internet would not give her any answers.

So be it. If feet on pavement was what it took, that's what it would take.

First, she had to drive there. It was a day's drive, over ten hours, and there was no time like the present. She closed the bookstore and left early the next morning.

She had taken out the book from her purse after the funeral, placing it high in a closet. Tucked away in the dark, it felt safe. More importantly, she felt safe, with it out of sight, felt safer knowing it *couldn't see her.*

The thought had poked its way into Annie's mind, and she had tucked it away, and had stopped thinking about it, because if she had pulled at that thread, she might not leave at all, but instead call up Ted, sell the book, and never think about it again, letting the guilt of Brad's unanswered death fester for the rest of her life.

It wasn't her fault, it wasn't, she had warned him, and he had promised, promised he would leave the book alone. He had said he wouldn't read the book—

You promised, Brad, you promised me, and you didn't, and you died—

Annie dismissed her sudden anger at Brad, pushed it away. She didn't know who or what killed Brad. It couldn't be the book, it couldn't be, it was some maniac, some person who followed the book, and killed whoever read it—

But they left the book alone.

Wouldn't they take the book, if they wanted people to not read it? Or maybe it was some sort of perverse punishment, a test for those to read a forbidden book?

But it wasn't some dark, holy tome. It wasn't filled with forbidden knowledge. It was a choose your own adventure book, a book for kids. And sure, someone killing Fleming or Brad made some sort of sense, with their wounds, but how did that explain Eddie? He died of natural causes.

They don't know that. They just assumed that, because he had no apparent *wounds.*

Annie's mind spun round and round in circles as she

drove all day through Pennsylvania.

Before she left, she had pulled the book down from the closet, wrapped it in newspaper, taped it, and then tucked it into her purse. She didn't know why she did it, again, but she felt safer with that thin layer of newsprint around it.

But as she drove, she still felt it. It might as well have been a gun in her purse, the gun that Brad pulled and played Russian Roulette with, and lost.

She played podcasts, and music, and anything, but eventually the noise was worse than her thoughts, and she drove in silence.

She reached Jefferson Township after dark, small flurries dropping down and sticking to the pavement. The Township wasn't big, with a population under ten thousand, but its city limits bled out into other surrounding suburbs, a morass that Annie didn't have a good read on. She had rented an AirBnb right outside the tiny downtown, and on the way through she had spotted a diner, Steve's Spoon, and made it her first stop after she had checked into her AirBnb.

The diner was bright in the dim evening, and had only a few guests when she stopped in, an hour before closing. A waitress named LouAnn with dirty blonde hair who looked to be in her 30s led her to a booth, and Annie ordered pancakes before the waitress left. She was hungry, and pancakes and syrup felt right.

Ten minutes later LouAnn dropped off the pancakes.

"Anything else you need?" she asked, as a matter of kind.

"Actually—" started Annie. "Are you from here?"

LouAnn cocked her eyebrow. "Yeah, I guess. Why?"

"I'm visiting. I'm looking for someone."

"Uh—"

"It's nothing bad, I promise. I'm trying to track down a Judy Sullivan. You wouldn't happen to know her, would you?"

LouAnn looked confused for a second, before shaking her head. "Never heard of her."

"She'd be much older than you."

"My grandma died when I was little," she said. "Only way I'd know any old timers. Hey, wait a second." LouAnn went behind the counter, and talked into the kitchen. The cook came over, and they spoke for a second. Annie took the opportunity to smother her pancakes in syrup.

LouAnn returned. "Phil doesn't know her either, but we're the same age. He had an idea, though. Said you should talk to Grease. He's older than us, and he knows everyone. Town historian."

"The town historian's name is Grease?"

"He's a mechanic," said LouAnn. "Runs Grease and Axle. I don't know his real name." She turned, and yelled at the kitchen. "Hey Phil, what's Grease's real name?"

"Howard!" yelled the cook.

"His real name is Howard," said LouAnn.

"You think he'll know?"

"He should," said LouAnn. "If anyone still alive knows where your Judy Sullivan is, he will."

"Thanks for your help," said Annie, smiling. LouAnn left, and Annie ate her pancakes, paid, and left a nice tip.

*

"I'll talk to you if you buy me lunch," was what Grease had said, when Annie had walked up to him in the late morning, his head buried under the hood of a minivan that was at least twenty years old. His hands were stained with grease, even when they were clean, and his gray hair threatened to turn white any day. White stubble covered his face from a three-day-old shave, but his eyes were golden and sharp, alien eyes on a pedestrian face.

"Call me Grease, don't call me Howard," was the only other thing he said before they sat down at Steve's Spoon, making Annie's second meal there in less than 24 hours. LouAnn served them again and winked at Annie as she took their orders. Grease got his usual, which turned out to be a BLT with extra mayo and french fries. Annie ordered a Frisco melt. It sounded good, and she wanted something hot with the cold outside.

"You drove all the way here?" asked Grease.

"Yes. Ten hours."

"That's a long drive," said Grease. "I'm not much for driving."

"Yet you fix cars."

"Yeah, funny, huh?" asked Grease. Their food came shortly, and Grease took a big bite of his BLT, the mayo dripping down the sides.

"Mike Sullivan was a horrible cunt," said Grease, finally, after swallowing down a chunk of tomato.

"You knew him?"

"Yeah, I knew him," said Grease. "Everyone my age knew him. He made sure of it."

"What does that mean?"

"He was an asshole, and a loud one," said Grease. "He made his goddamn money, and he threw his weight around. Anywhere he went in town, if anyone gave him shit, or even threatened to, he would make sure they knew he was in charge."

"Was he in charge?"

"No," said Grease. "But he had money, and he could afford to make your life hard, if he didn't like you. And he didn't like anyone."

"Why?"

"That's a good question," said Grease. "His dad was also a horrible cunt. That has something to do with it, I'm sure. And losing his kids. And Judy's health. It all added up." Grease took another bite, chewed, swallowed. "But I only knew him after. So excuse me if I'm not kind to his memory."

"His kids? And what happened to Judy?"

"The kids were killed in some accident," he said. "Like I said, before my time. It was a town legend when I was growing up. Judy, I think it was congenital. Something in her back, I don't know."

"Do you know how he died?"

"No," said Grease. "No one does. Except for Judy, maybe. We didn't throw a party when he died—but no one shed a tear. They didn't have a funeral, but if they did, no one would have gone. Again, except for Judy."

"Anything strange about his death?"

"There were rumors," said Grease. "Of course there were. He hadn't been seen in quite a while before, either. Some people even speculated it was Judy who did it, to get insurance money. But ain't no way. Judy loved him. Only one who did."

"Did people hate Judy, too?"

"No," said Grease, swallowing another bite. The BLT was

almost gone. "We all pitied her. And she was the only way to get through to him. Only way to *ever* get Mike to call off his dogs was to talk to Judy. When she could get away with it."

"Get away with it?"

"Mike didn't like her talking to too many people," said Grease. "In his mind, he was protecting her, I'm sure. But all it did was strangle her."

"Is she still alive?"

Grease swallowed the last piece of his BLT and looked at her. "As far as I know. If you want to call it living."

"Where is she?"

"There's a retirement home," said Grease. "Couple miles away. Golden Sunset, it's called. She's there."

A small spark of hope lit inside Annie. Judy was alive and was nearby. Maybe she could get answers from her.

"You think she'll talk to me?"

"Probably not," said Grease, his oil stained hand filled with french fries. He dipped them in the mayo that had fallen off his sandwich. Annie's heart sank.

"Why?"

"As far as I know, she hasn't said a word to anyone since Mike died," said Grease, looking at her, his beautiful, golden eyes staring into hers. "Not a peep." He chewed and swallowed a mass of fries. He eyed her sandwich. "You gonna eat that?"

12

The Golden Sunset Retirement Home was built over forty years ago, and the owners did their best to hide its age.

The landscaping was immaculate, well kept up, with trees and hedges trimmed, with mulch and flowers planted. New coats of paint covered the outside of the extensive building, three stories tall. The moulding, the siding, the fascia, all had been painted a fresh coat of navy blue, and it helped.

But it couldn't cover up the old windows. Single pane, the paint sealing them shut. Or the sagging roof. Or the aging pagoda that stood in front of the building, empty, and half collapsed.

The inside was much the same. It was clean and smelled of antiseptic, of bleach, of ammonia. They did a good job of keeping it clean, but cleaning only removed certain things.

Some filth was impossible to excise, and the edges of the linoleum floors and the curling wallpaper revealed that certain things couldn't be fixed without a full scale gutting of the building, and renovating.

But with that came cost, and it was clear the owners wouldn't be footing the bill.

"I'm here to see Judy Sullivan," said Annie, with as much confidence as she could muster. It was visiting hours, and their website had made no mention if only friends and family were welcome, but she didn't volunteer a relation.

"Mrs. Sullivan?" asked the nurse, a stout middle-aged woman, who wore bright red lipstick. "You're here to see Judy?"

"Yes," said Annie, mustering a smile.

"Can I ask how you know her?"

"My mother was friends with her, long ago," said Annie. "I've been reconnecting with them. I tracked down Judy, and wanted to say hello. To see how she's doing."

The nursed eyed her for a moment, her face doubtful. Annie's story was paper thin, and if the nurse poked at it, she'd punch holes right through. Her face remained questioning for just a moment, and Annie desperately ignored the worry in her stomach, and then the nurse smiled and stood up.

"That sounds so lovely," said the nurse. "I wish more people would do the same. Follow me. Let's see if we can track down Judy. But I'd bet I know where she is."

The nurse stood up and gestured for Annie to follow. The fluorescent lights overhead hummed as they delved into the bowels of the facility. They passed resident's rooms and recreation areas and the cafeteria, where some residents ate a late breakfast, scattered around large, round tables, watching the news on a huge flatscreen bolted to the wall.

"Judy doesn't get visitors," said the nurse.

"Ever?"

"Not since I've worked here," she said. "And I've been here for the past four years. I hope—hope that she'll be happy to see you."

Annie thought to question the hesitance in her voice, but said nothing.

"I think she's in the second common room. It's where she usually sits—" said the nurse, leading Annie through propped open double doors into another space, empty except for a couple of couches thrown against the walls, and a few more of the big round tables that stood in the middle of the area, lined with chairs. A flatscreen was mounted in the corner.

"There she is, right where I thought she'd be," said the nurse, and Annie saw Judy Sullivan, sitting in a wheelchair, pulled up to the table, her head back, vacantly staring at the news, the volume loud. Judy was small, her back contorted and crooked. Her face was wrinkled, her hair white and tousled on her head. Her eyes, though, were dark blue, almost black.

"Mrs. Sullivan?" asked the nurse, trying to get her attention. Judy only stared at the TV. "This is Annie. She's here to visit you." The nurse gestured to the seat nearest Judy. Annie took it, Judy still not looking at either of them.

The nurse grabbed the remote and turned off the television.

"So you two can talk," said the nurse. "If you need anything, just shout." She smiled at Annie and then left them alone. Judy still stared at the empty television.

Silence lingered in the room, the smell of ammonia wafting into Annie's nostrils. Her nose burned from the chemicals. She set the pain aside.

"Hi, Judy," said Annie, extending a hand toward her. "My name is Annie Maddox. I'm doing some research on your husband, Mike, and I'd love to interview you about him, his work, and his life."

Judy's eyes left the television then, darting toward Annie, and Annie had to stop herself from jumping. Judy's eyes stared at her, but they were unreadable. Annie gave her a minute, but Judy said nothing.

"Do you not want to talk?" asked Annie. Judy only stared at her. "Or can you *not* talk?"

Annie looked at her and sat in silence. It was a trick she learned in college. If you wanted someone else to speak, the trick wasn't to talk more, to plead, or cajole. It was to be silent and use it to pull the other person into filling it.

But Judy didn't fill the silence. She only stared. Minutes passed, and Annie realized Judy was waiting her out. The quiet wouldn't coax anything out of Judy.

"Grease said you haven't said a word since Mike's death," said Annie. "What did you see, Judy?" Judy's eyes still stared down Annie, but now they wavered. Annie took a small breath, waiting.

Still nothing.

You have to show her. It's the only way.

Annie exhaled, inhaled, and then exhaled. So be it. She laid her purse on the table and reached inside, grabbing the wrapped copy of *The Mystery of the Sentinel Lodge*. Judy's eyes shifted from Annie to the book, widening.

Annie carefully unwrapped it, tucking the newspaper back into her purse. She'd need it again. Judy stared daggers at the paperback.

"I heard they found this with Mike's body," said Annie. "The only copy of his last book." She set it on the table in front of Judy, the cover facing her. "Is that true?"

Judy looked away then, her gaze finally breaking. But still, no answer.

Talk, damn you. You know something.

Annie leaned in toward her. "Did this book kill your husband, Judy? I need to know. I *need* to know."

Judy finally looked back at her, her eyes wavering again, the dark black-blue shining.

"How did you get that?" asked Judy, her voice a hoarse whisper.

Annie took a breath, collecting herself. "I bought it, along with a friend. We ran a bookstore together. It was in an estate sale."

Judy pursed her lips, looking at the book again.

"Your friend is dead, isn't he?" asked Judy, her eyes casting up, back to Annie.

Annie felt tears coming, and she forced her eyes shut, and pushed them back. She wouldn't cry, not now. She would save those tears for later, when she had the time. Annie nodded.

"Yes," said Annie. "One man dead, the estate sale. A second, who tried to take the book from us. A third, my friend. All found holding the book. It's impossible. But it's not a coincidence. It can't be. This book did it. It carries some curse."

"How did they die?" asked Judy, her voice a low and dark rumble, shaking her withered body.

Annie opened her eyes, the tears gone. "The first, apparently of natural causes. The second—and third—both dead from an attack. Some weapon, to the face, head, and body. Sharp. No evidence left behind. Just—nothing."

"There wouldn't be," said Judy. "At least not here."

"Not here?"

Judy nodded at the book. "It's in there, if there's anything."

"*In* the book?" asked Annie. "I don't understand."

"Yes, you do," said Judy, a terse, slim smile on her face. "You've come this far, so you already know. You just don't want to acknowledge it, because it's too far. It breaks all the rules, the ones you've known your whole life. And if you try and tell anyone about it, they'll think you're crazy. And not just a little bit. They'll think you're *committed* crazy. They thought I was. After a while, I stopped trying to explain what happened. They wouldn't believe me. Why bother?"

"What happened to you, Judy? What happened to Mike? What happened to my friend?" asked Annie, her voice desperate.

Judy leaned back into her wheelchair, as much as her body would allow, and took a deep breath, and exhaled, a harsh noise.

"I loved Mike. I did. Maybe the only one who ever did. His dad didn't love him, that's for sure. He could be a miserable man. Hard to the world. He'd had to cut his empathy off at the knees for years and years, and even after I tried to nurture it back to health, it was slow going. And after we lost Sam and Joanie—well, I think he lost that, too."

"Grease said everyone hated him."

"He gave them reason," said Judy. She paused. "But he

took care of me, when no one else would, or could." She gestured to her body. "Even when I was young, my back—I couldn't work. Couldn't support myself. And my parents had no interest in helping me after I became an adult. Maybe it's what drew Mike to me, or vice versa. Our parents. We both had to survive without them. He—he structured his life around caring for me." Judy stopped. "Would you get me some water? It's been a long time since I've spoken this much."

Annie spotted a water cooler in the corner, with a stack of cups on top. She filled a cup to the top and returned, setting it on the table near Judy.

"Thank you," said Judy, grasping the cup with gnarled fingers and slowly sipping at it. She took a breath. "I think it's what hurt him the most."

"What?"

"How little the world cared for me," said Judy. "The disparity. And it still hurts me. That our love was the source of so much of his bitterness."

"Judy—"

"I'm telling you all this because it matters," said Judy. "And I don't think you'll ever speak to me again after this. So I'd like for you to have a complete picture of Mike, before you leave. He was a monster, yes, but he was *my* monster. You understand?"

"Yes."

"I softened him, I did. But honestly, it was the twins. Sam and Joanie." She smiled. "They did most of the work, just by existing. Mike always worked best when he had a purpose. To protect me. To raise the kids." A tear flowed down her cheek. She wiped it away. "Those were the best times. When they were little. Mike's writing was making good money. We were happy."

"I was told there was an accident," said Annie. Judy's face contorted in sadness, just for a moment, and then returned to normal. A brief window into terrible grief.

"Yes," said Judy. "Mike blamed himself. It wasn't his fault. Sometimes, bad things happen, and you can't stop it. But he was never the same. And it all cascaded from there. My back got worse. And his writing contracts dried up."

"The choose your own adventure books?"

Judy nodded. "He wrote because it let him stay home with me. He could send in his books to the publisher, collect a paycheck, and not have to drive out into the world every day. He was good at it, but it wasn't a passion. It was a means to an end. He was efficient, and wrote quickly, and wrote whatever would sell. And that led him to choose your own adventure books."

She took another sip.

"They sold well," said Judy. "Made us money. More than we needed, but not as much we wanted. The contracts Mike got for that work weren't great, but your hands were tied back then. But they did well, for a time. His career—he always described it as a maze. With no solution."

"What happened?"

Judy nodded. "They took it all from him."

"What do you mean?"

"The publisher sold the rights to all his books to another publisher, who put them all under a single choose your own adventure brand. They cut out Mike. They hired ghost writers, who kept publishing under the old names. He didn't get anything from it. It was his first taste of success, and it was gone in a second. And there was nothing he could do. And—“

Judy stopped then, her eyes gleaming. She closed them once, and opened them, and they were hard again, dark black-blue and cold.

“And that was the beginning of the end. Mike couldn’t write anymore. He would treat it like a normal job. He’d clock in, clock out, nine to five. But no words would come, not after that. And he blamed the publishers. But more than that. He blamed the world.”

“That still doesn’t explain this,” said Annie, her fingers grazing the cover of the book, and Judy’s eyes opened wide with fear.

“Don’t do that,” said Judy. “Don’t touch it. You should wrap it up again.” Her eyes stayed on it, and Annie grabbed the newspaper, and wrapped the book, and tucked it back into her purse. Judy calmed.

“Mike sank into darkness. He wasn’t just miserable. He became a—a bastard. There’s no other way to describe it. It was the only time in his life the nastiness ever bled onto me. And it was the first time in my life that I ever hated him. But I persevered. I didn’t stop loving him, at the same time. I hoped he would pull through.” Judy took a halting breath. “And he did pull through. And that book is the result.”

“I don’t understand.”

“By then, there was an early internet,” said Judy. “Mike had never really liked the computer, but he spent more and more time on it. He told me he had found a bulletin board, a message board, to talk to people. And he’d found some like-minded folk. Those were the words he used. ‘Like-minded folk.’ And at first, it was just that. Him spending more and more time, glued to the screen, typing back and forth." Judy took a sip. "But it didn't stay that way. Soon, he was going out, and meeting up with them. And Mike, he didn't like leaving the house. Even trips to the grocery story, to the post office. He hated it. At first, I was happy. He had made friends."

Judy smiled then, a true smile, that vanished in an instant.

"He started writing again. The darkness had lifted, I thought." She paused. "But it hadn't. Something worse had settled in. That book was the product."

Judy stared at Annie's bag, at the small piece of the book that stuck out of the top of her purse. Her gaze stayed on it.

Annie tucked it all the way in, so it couldn't be seen. "There's something you're not telling me."

Judy stared at her again. "I never met those men. I couldn't leave the house, not without Mike's help, and he would *never* let me meet them, not even after months. And I let it be. But they did something to that book. I don't know what, I don't know how, but they gave it power."

"What power? What happened to you, Judy? What happened to Mike?"

Judy swallowed the last of the water, and stared at Annie, hard, not blinking. "He read the book, and it killed him."

"How? How?"

"We were there," said Judy. "He read it at home. Maybe he didn't know. Maybe he didn't believe that it would work. But he read the book, and we were there."

"There? I don't—"

"Yes, you do," said Judy. "You already suspected, but something in your mind stopped you from finishing the thought." She took a breath. "We were in the Sentinel Lodge. We became the book. We were transported into that world. A world of deadly ghosts, of murderous caretakers, of a haunted lodge. We were transported there—or—or our world became theirs? I don't know. But we were there, and Mike died, killed by something in there. I don't know what. I didn't have my wheelchair. Mike—he hid me in a closet, and made me promise not to come out." She paused. "All I heard was him screaming, a piercing, horrible noise, that I had never heard before. And I heard—"

"What did you hear?"

Judy shook her head. "It—it doesn't matter. But it happened."

"That's impossible,."

"Yes," said Judy. "But it's true. If you read that book, it takes you. And then it kills you."

Annie stared at Judy, reading her face. There was no deceit there. Judy believed.

"You went to the Sentinel Lodge?"

"Yes," said Judy. "I was there for an hour, as Mike evaded whatever hells he wrote in that adventure. But then he died—and—and I came back. Back where I left off, the only evidence was Mike's corpse and my memory."

She took a deep, halting breath, and fell into silence.

"There has to be more," said Annie. "What did they do to the book, to give it that power? Why did Mike read it?"

"I don't know," said Judy. "No one believed my story, so I stopped telling it. But I couldn't support myself, not without Mike, and we had no savings. My niece keeps me here, which I should be thankful for. I'd be on the street, otherwise."

"You never found any trace of what Mike did when he left the house? Who he met with?"

Judy's eyes went to Annie.

"Of course I did," said Judy.

"And?"

"And what?" asked Judy. "I'm trapped, Annie. I had a wheelchair, but no one to push it. I called them, over and over again. Left messages. No one answered. They hid. They scattered like rats. And that was 30 years ago."

"Do you still have their information?"

Judy only stared again, silent.

"Judy—"

"Of course," said Judy.

"Will you—"

"Forget this. All of it."

"Judy, I can't—"

"I know, your friend," said Judy. "You want answers. And despite everything you've seen so far, and everything I've told you, you're still not sure if you believe me. And even if you do, you think of it like Narnia. Like a trip through a wardrobe. But it's nothing of the kind. That book will only bring you pain. Get rid of it, forget about it. Move on. It's the only advice I have."

Judy stared, and Annie stared right back.

"I'll give you the information," said Judy. "It's in my room. But please, be careful. Anyone connected to those men—they're dangerous. And please. Please—don't read that book. Ever."

13

Annie extended her stay in the AirBnb.

Judy had given her all the info she had, an old notebook half-filled with scrawled email addresses, discontinued phone numbers, and all the information she had found about the small circle of men that Mike had befriended over the early internet.

Annie started over, compiling the loose and messy notebook into something she could use. She started with their names.

Mike Sullivan
Kevin Newman
Owen Jenkins
Bob Harper

Sean Reading
Ellis Thompson

She knew what had happened to Mike.

No, you don't, only what Judy told you—

Annie forced those thoughts out of her head. She wasn't ready to reckon with that, not yet.

Judy had only found dead ends searching for the five other men, and as Annie flipped through the notebook and compiled all of Judy's info into docs on her laptop, Annie thought that was only a metaphor.

But as she followed each man through Judy's scribbles, she realized it wasn't a metaphor.

Every man had died.

DEAD wrote Judy, sometime in the past, at the bottom of the page after digging into Owen Jenkins, sleuthing her way past an email and phone number, finding an address, and then those four capital letters scrawled hastily at the bottom.

Annie transcribed everything to her laptop, giving each of the men a document, and writing down everything Judy had discovered. Soon there was nothing left in the notebook, no information Annie hadn't digested.

But the fact remained. All of them, dead. A couple had causes of death, written next to them. But for the rest, just an ominous proclamation.

Kevin Newman had died in a car accident.

Ellis had committed suicide.

But no other causes of death, aside from Mike himself.

Sentinel Lodge hadn't killed them. No book was found in their hands. As far as she knew, the book's ownership had arced away from this group.

Could it be a coincidence?

It was possible. But Annie didn't buy it. Whatever connected these men had led to them all dying.

But it wasn't the book that killed them.

Unless they all had a copy?

Annie pushed that thought away. She would follow the information she had, and let her conclusion come from something she could nail down, with concrete facts.

Like a cursed choose your own adventure book?

Annie didn't confront the thought, not yet. But she knew that if there was a door that represented her belief in the power of the book, where it was once shut tight, it was now ajar. And with every piece of information she found, it swung further open. Annie only worried that if she acknowledged it, that her sanity might disappear alongside it, through that open door.

Find your answers first, Annie. Worry about your sanity later.

Annie had access to something that Judy didn't. The modern internet, with the wide range of easily accessible data.

Judy had addresses for five of the six men, and with a little internet sleuthing, Annie found the sixth, for Sean Reading. She created a GPS map of all of their addresses. All of them were in Pennsylvania, but it was a big state, and they were quite far apart.

She looked up their names online, specifically keyed to where they lived. Looking for any info on archived local newspapers.

Annie didn't find much. Sean Reading had been a volunteer fireman.

Kevin Newman had owned a small restaurant in his town, which had sponsored a chili cook-off.

Minute details about their lives. Tiny windows into their worlds. But all of it was quite old, nothing newer than the early 90s, right about when Judy had mentioned the "like-minded folk" had met online, in some chat room or bulletin board.

There wasn't much, except for their obituaries.

She found those, easily enough, for all the men. With them, she could piece together a little more. Most had families. Only Bob Harper was single. The four who were married, aside from Mike, all had children.

Annie typed it all out, building out dossiers for each of the men.

She had phone numbers for all of them. She called.

Three of five were disconnected, with no answer whatsoever. One was a wrong number, with the young man on the other end having no idea who Bob Harper was. The sixth answered.

"Hello, Marjorie Thompson speaking."

Annie was slightly stunned with someone answering. She forced herself to speak.

"Hi, I'm looking for information on Ellis Thompson. Are you related to him?"

There was a long pause. "He was my husband."

Annie had rehearsed what she would say in her head, but now confronted with an actual person, her tongue wasn't cooperating.

"Well, hello. I'm Annie Maddox, and I was researching Mike Sullivan. In the process, I have discovered a circle of friends that Mike had made, with your late husband being a part of it. I've been trying to track down what exactly—"

CLICK.

"Ms. Thompson?" asked Annie and then realized she'd been hung up on. Annie thought to call her back, but what would that achieve? Annie was back exactly where Judy had been. She had more information, to a certain extent, but no one would talk to her, and all the men were dead.

What else could she learn? She was left with what she started with. That this book was cursed, and killed her friend.

Annie stared at the GPS map. The six dots were the six men, all dead. Three were clustered near Pittsburgh, within an hour of where she was now. One of those was Mike.

Another was in the suburbs of Philadelphia, over a five-hour drive. Another was north of her, in the northwest corner of the state, and the last was north central, a few hours from her.

Annie felt the urge to pull open her bank app on her phone, and look at how much she had left. She resisted the urge. She knew how much there had been, how *little* remained, with the bookstore's rent due at the end of the month. Annie couldn't play private detective forever. The real world would come calling.

Go home. Sell the book. Forget it.

It was the smart thing to do. But she hadn't exhausted every possibility. Until she had, she would push on and pull every penny from her bank account. She had her credit cards. They could bear it, for now.

She stared at the map again. Two of them were close, within an hour's drive. She'd go to those first, and then the address north of her, only a couple more hours away. After that—well, she'd see what she found first.

*

Getting up first thing in the morning, she could hit all three in a single, long day of driving.

First up was Sean Reading, only twenty-five minutes away.

The neighborhood wasn't too different from the one the AirBnb was in, filled with a mixture of old homes and renovated ones, having been flipped over the years and the subsequent real estate booms.

Reading's former home looked older, with outdoor fixtures not out of place from the 90s. Annie parked in front, and taking a deep breath, walked up to the front door. She knocked once, and then twice, and just as she was about to knock again, she heard footsteps from inside.

The door opened a crack, and Annie saw a security chain, still attached on the inside. An older woman peeked out from inside, the distant sounds of a television filtering out to Annie.

"How can I help you?" asked the woman.

"Hi, did you know a Sean Reading?" asked Annie.

The woman stared at Annie, her eyes creasing into worry. "Yes. He was my brother."

Annie took in a breath, hoping the air would help soothe the ache in her stomach. She forced a smile.

"Hi, my name is Annie Maddox. I was doing research on the late author Mike Sullivan, and I found evidence of an online friend group he had fostered, which included your late brother. I was wondering if I could come in and talk to you about him."

Reading's sister hesitated, her mind parsing the information.

"I'm sorry, what is this all for?"

"Well, like I said, I was doing a research project on Mike Sullivan—what's your name?" Annie asked.

"Beth," she said, still staring through the crack of the door.

"Beth, it's a long story, but a friend and I had come into possession of this book—" and Annie pulled out the wrapped paperback, hoping it would open the door.

Beth's eyes snapped to it, and Annie recognized the emotion in them.

Fear.

"No, no," she said, almost inaudible, and shut the door.

Annie stood on the doorstep and sighed. She knocked again.

"Please, Beth, I've come very far to talk to you," said Annie. "My friend is dead. I just want—I just want answers."

There was a silence on the other side of the door, and Annie knew she still stood there.

"Please," said Annie.

More silence, and finally Beth spoke. "I've answered enough questions about Sean. They closed the case. Please leave."

Annie took another deep breath. *Closed what case?*

She knocked again. "Beth, please!"

"Please leave. I will call the police," said Beth.

Annie went to knock again, and then dropped her hand. She took another deep breath and walked back to her car.

*

The second stop was another half hour to the east, farther from the city. Annie pulled up to the curb and parked in front of the house.

Or what was left of it.

The house had once been a fairly standard mid-century built home, but time had destroyed it. The windows were boarded up, and two beaten up cars were parked in the driveway, all eight tires flat, with registration on both ten years expired.

It had been a long time since someone had lived here.

Annie got out and went to the front door, with glances to the left and right down the street. The neighborhood was a little more rundown than the last, but still, there was an array of nice houses, with luxury cars in the driveway. Owen Jenkins' old house was the exception.

PREMISES UNDER 24 HOUR SURVEILLANCE read a sign plastered to the door. Annie's eyes swept around the front door, and under the eaves to the right and left, all the usual places for a security camera. There were no cameras, only the sign warning of them.

Annie assumed no one lived there and tried the door.

It was unlocked, and she pushed her way in, the hinges creaking as she entered.

The interior looked worse than the exterior. The hardwood floors were no doubt once beautiful, but water damage and lack of care had ruined them. The floors sagged in spots, with massive holes in others, collapsing underneath the house.

Annie looked around in the dim, ruined house, trying to get a sense of what Jenkins' life was like, and what led to his death.

Why had she come in here? She had thought, that maybe, she could find some clues to his death in here, some way to find what happened to him and his family, but there was nothing but rot and ruin. Annie looked down, and saw other shoeprints in the dust and dirt, and realized that she wasn't the only person who had entered the house, and a sense of danger suddenly pierced her heart. She heard a shuffling noise from deeper inside.

Annie retreated, hurrying back to her vehicle. Her eyes looked to the front door again, from inside her car, the doors locked, but it didn't move.

*

The house in northwest Pennsylvania was two hours away, and Annie arrived shortly after lunchtime, stopping at a drive-through for a quick sandwich.

She scanned through the radio on the way, jumping between stations, avoiding commercials. Avoiding silence.

It's another dead end, Annie. Another shut door. Another abandoned house. More tragedy, with no answers. Go home. Sell the book. Forget it.

But Annie didn't, and in a couple hours' time, pulled up to the third address, the former home of Kevin Newman. The house wasn't boarded up, with an SUV parked in the driveway, a few years old. The house wasn't renovated, but looked kept up.

Still, Annie's expectations were low. She took a deep

breath and walked up to the front door, not letting her guts give out before she could do it. There was a modern security doorbell, and she pushed the lit up button. She heard it ring inside once, twice, and then a voice came from behind the camera.

"Hello, how can I help you?" asked a female voice.

"Hi, my name is Annie Maddox. I was researching Mike Sullivan—"

"Say that again."

Annie paused. "I was researching Mike Sullivan, and discovered he used to be friends with a man who once lived here, a Kevin Newman."

A long pause. "Do you have the item?"

Item? The book?

"What do you mean?" asked Annie, staring into the doorbell.

"Do you have his book?"

Annie paused. Whoever this was, they knew about the book.

"I—I—yes, yes I do," said Annie. She went to reach into her purse.

"No, don't," said the voice. "Wait a second." There was a click, and the call hung up.

A few moments later, a deadbolt slid aside and the door opened. A petite black-haired woman stood on the other side. She stared at Annie, considering her. She spoke.

"We should talk."

14

It feels like an Ikea showroom.

It was Annie's first thought, as she followed the woman into her home. The house was nice inside, clean, well kept, minimally decorated.

Annie had the same coffee table, and looking around, she recognized all the furniture from her trips to Ikea.

The woman walked to the living room and sat down in a blue armchair, gesturing to the couch.

"Please, have a seat," said the woman, awkwardly. Annie felt like she was on a talk show, without an audience in sight. "Can I get you some water?"

"Not right now," said Annie, sitting down, holding her purse close to her. The weight of the book inside felt heavy.

"I'm Minerva Jordan," she said, not extending a hand.

"I'm Kevin Newman's daughter." Annie's eyes darted to Minerva's fingers. There were no rings. She eyed Minerva. Minerva's voice was quiet, but she was articulate, and seemed to weigh each word on its way out of her.

"Why—"

"The name difference?" asked Minerva. "I had my name changed. It's complicated. Maybe you'll understand, eventually."

"I—well, I came here—"

Minerva studied her, her large, dark green eyes staring intently. Annie stopped.

"I don't know how to start," said Annie. "I came here looking for answers."

"Answers about the book?"

"Well, yes," said Annie. "But not just that. My friend—" Annie felt emotion well up in her again, and she stopped, and forced it back down.

"He died," said Minerva, not a question.

"Yes," said Annie. "We bought the book, on accident, really. We're booksellers. We were working on a deal to sell it, and then he was dead, killed. And not the only one."

Minerva nodded, her face plain. It wasn't dismissive, but there was no surprise. It bore the same staid sadness it had when she first opened the door.

"Can I have that water, now?"

"Sure," said Minerva, who got up and filled a glass in the kitchen, and brought it over. Annie took and drank. Her throat was suddenly parched, and she realized the glasses were Ikea as well. Minerva sat back down.

"Is everything in your house from Ikea?"

"Yes," said Minerva, allowing herself a slight smile. "It's

easier that way." She paused, and before Annie could ask what that meant, she spoke again. "I've done what you're doing."

"What does that mean?"

"You have a list, of six men," said Minerva. "Emails. Phone numbers. You've pieced it together and got their home addresses. You're visiting them, talking to surviving family, piecing together what happened to these six men. How did they all die? And if it's all because of that book, that's presumably in your purse."

"How do you know that?" asked Annie, staring.

"That's what I'm saying," said Minerva. "I did the same thing. I tracked them all down. I spoke to whoever would speak to me. I kept notes, and worked my way through a web of lost knowledge and tragedy."

Silence hung in the room. Annie stared.

"Well?" asked Annie. "Are you going to tell me?"

Minerva finally broke eye contact. She sighed. "I'll tell you whatever you want to know. But you won't like it. I'm sure you have questions about the book. What do you know about it?"

Annie thought to it, so close to her. She could feel it, inside her purse, in her arms.

"I know of three deaths, including my friend, who were found with it in their hands. They all read the book, I'm convinced. I spoke to Judy Sullivan. She said the book killed Mike. That it transported both of them to the Sentinel Lodge, the setting of the story. That it killed Mike, and she came survived. She believes the book is alive, somehow. And that whoever reads it will die."

Minerva said nothing, finally looking back at Annie.

"What do *you* believe?"

"I don't know!" said Annie, raising her voice, the emotion bubbling up again, but it wasn't sadness. It was frustration. "I don't know what to believe! It doesn't make any sense. Judy didn't think she was lying to me. She believed every word. My friend Brad is dead, and two others, just in the time I've known about the book. And the author, and the five other men who were connected, all dead. Too many coincidences. Something is going on, but I don't know what. If it does kill, why would anyone read it? Has it just stumbled into everyone's path? Is this book magic? Is it cursed?"

With that word, Minerva's eyes lit up, with a spark. Annie took another sip of water, attempting to calm herself.

"I'm sorry for raising my voice—"

"You don't have to apologize," said Minerva. "I feel the same way."

"You seem pretty calm."

"Well, it's taken a lot of work on my part," said Minerva. "Also, I'm a little desensitized. But you have a right to be angry, to be frustrated. Encountering the items is challenging. It challenges our concept of the world."

"I don't understand," said Annie. "Wait—*items?* Are there more copies of the book?"

Minerva shook her head. "No, you have the only copy. But there were six men. And there are six items. Six cursed items."

"Six of them?" asked Annie. Her mind boggled. "Okay, wait. The book is cursed?"

"How else would you describe it?" asked Minerva. "Corrupted? Possessed? Cursed is simpler, and as accurate as we can be."

"But how? And why? And where are the other five items?"

Minerva sat silently for a moment, and then answered. "I have two of them."

"What?" asked Annie. "Where?"

"I'd prefer not to say," said Minerva. "But they're safe, somewhere no one will ever find them."

"Can you tell me what they are?" asked Annie. "You said—"

"I'm sorry," said Minerva. "Let me start over. It'll make things simpler. We jumped directly into the deep end." She took a heavy breath, the simple sadness evident on her face again. "I miss my dad."

"What happened?" asked Annie.

She sat silent. "I know it's not my fault," said Minerva, finally. "I cannot and could not center my life around someone else's needs. I have to satisfy my own first. But me leaving home started it all for him. My mom died when I was very little. My dad raised me on his own. And he was a good dad. Was he perfect? Of course not, no one is. But he was kind, and supportive, and did everything he could for me." Minerva sighed. "He was lonely, I think. In the end, I think it was just loneliness."

"Judy had told me Mike could be a cruel man. Everyone I talked to said the same thing."

"The six men were all very different from each other. But all of them desperately searched for kinship. Fellowship, even. And it started with that. All of them felt alone, and powerless. They all smoked cigars. That was the shared interest. It was a cigar forum on usenet, in the early internet. And they would meet and smoke cigars. Drive across the state, in some instances."

"That seems innocent," said Annie. "How did it turn into curses?"

"All evidence points to Ellis Thompson being the man who found it. He had occult interest, from what I could find. I can't confirm it, though. It doesn't matter. But I suspect it was him, who found the information. On how to conduct the ritual. On what each man needed to bring. On how it worked, and what it would give them."

"What ritual?"

"I don't have any direct sources," said Minerva. "I don't think Ellis had only one source, either. He was a folklorist. He had compiled data from several places. I don't know what, though. If he shared them with the group, there's no evidence of it. But he had information, of a ritual, an old one, that he thought would imbue objects with power. And he convinced the rest of the group to buy in."

"What do you mean? Magic?"

"Sure," said Minerva. "That word works well enough. From my father's notes, Ellis had said that something powerful from the old world was brought into the new. That these forces converged, and brought about a new thing. Something big, and powerful, something that could be tapped into if you knew how."

"What does that mean?" asked Annie. "Gods? Demons?"

"I don't know," said Minerva.

"What ritual? How did they do it? *Where* did they do it?"

"I don't know."

"You said you've already followed this path."

"I have," said Minerva. "But there's only so much information to go around. I found everything I could, but nothing detailed the ritual. At least nothing left. Ellis's widow destroyed everything he had used. It's probably for the best. Even if the items can't be destroyed, at least no more items can be imbued."

"What?" asked Annie. "They can't be destroyed?"

"I've tried my best, with the two items I have," said Annie. "They seem invincible. So I gave up. I presume the rest are the same. They are intrinsic, now."

"What items do you have?"

"I have the gun, and the cigar," said Minerva. "You have the book. Three others. A car. A wallet. A dog."

"A dog?" asked Annie. "A living dog?"

Minerva pressed her lips together and nodded. "My father took specific notes about the six items. It's how I acquired the two I have. I knew what to look for. Owen Jenkins was a hunter. He brought a rifle, that once imbued, never missed its target. Jenkins used it to kill seven people, and then himself. He didn't miss. Ellis Thompson brought a cigar. Whoever smoked it would gain any knowledge they wanted. He smoked it, and lost his mind. Again, suicide. Bob Harper loved his car, more than anything in the world. Given power, it would take you wherever you wanted to go. It took him off a cliff. Sean Reading, a wallet, that always had the money you needed. Someone killed him for it."

"Jesus fucking Christ," said Annie. "Mike was the book. Your father—"

"The dog, yes," said Minerva. "When I went off to college, he got a dog. Do you like dogs?"

"Of course," said Annie. "Who doesn't like dogs?"

"Exactly," said Minerva. "My father had always wanted one. He rescued one. It was older, and filled a part of dad's loneliness. He loved it, with all his heart. But it had health problems, and he couldn't bear to lose it. So he gave it a long life. A life as long as his."

Annie's stomach dropped. "Did it—it didn't—?"

"Kill him?" asked Minerva. "No, not directly. They died together. A drunk driver crossed over onto the sidewalk and hit them on a late night walk."

"Then there are only five items, then," said Annie.

"They never found the dog," said Minerva. "Only my dad. I don't know. I don't know." Minerva stared down, and closed her eyes, and Annie realized that it was the first time she'd seen Minerva hold her eyes shut since they'd arrived.

"The book," said Annie, reaching for her purse.

"Don't," said Minerva. "Leave it there. You have it wrapped?"

"Yes."

"Good," said Minerva. "I don't want to see it."

"Okay," said Annie. "But all the other items, the six men—they all asked for something powerful. They all wished, and all they got was ironic fulfillment."

"Yes," said Minerva. "The book is no different."

"How?" asked Annie. "Mike was a bastard, by all accounts, but I don't see how it benefits him to create a book that kills people when they read it."

"Of course not," said Annie. "And Mike was smart. Maybe he saw it coming. Or, being burned by his past books being taken from him, he built in a safeguard. The power given to his book would be locked inside."

"And what was that?"

"To get whatever your heart desires," said Minerva. "Those are the exact words written by my father. But to get it, you would read through the book. Find the right ending, and you would win the prize. And obviously, Mike had written the book. He knew the right ending."

"But he died," said Annie. "Killed in the Sentinel Lodge."

"Yes," said Minerva. "The book killed him. Obviously, he didn't know the way. And there's no way of knowing, not anymore. The only man who would know was Mike. But my bet would be that the power also rewrote the book. Or—or maybe it struck the memory from Mike. He would have to go in blind." She paused. "I don't know."

"So this book will give me whatever my heart desires?"

"Maybe," said Minerva. "It's a wonder you've brought it back to me. But I wouldn't put it past the book to have worked its way back here on purpose."

"What does that mean?"

"All of these items killed their masters," said Minerva. "Whatever power is imbued into them, it is malevolent, and it is alive."

"They're alive? You're saying they're—sentient?"

"I think so," said Minerva. "When I'm in the presence of the items, I feel—different. Felt an urge to use a rifle, even though I'm strictly against guns of all types. Felt the urge to smoke the cigar, so I would know the knowledge I so desperately craved. I knew if I used them, I would die. But they affected me. Whatever power is in them, it influences those around it."

Annie closed her eyes and rubbed the bridge of her nose. She felt a headache developing. This was too much information, and she didn't know how to parse it all.

"You still don't believe, do you?" asked Minerva.

"It's so much," said Annie. "It's several leaps of logic,

of believing things I've never believed, and in some cases, thought were squarely impossible. Magic, and old gods. Rituals. Curses. I don't know—"

"What to do," said Minerva. "I know. I faced the same problem. How do I continue on, with these items, so inextricably connected to my life? With my father, killed by them?"

Annie looked into Minerva's eyes. There was a confidence there. Maybe it had always been there, and Annie hadn't recognized it.

"What should I do?" asked Annie.

"You can give me the book."

"What will you do with it?"

"Keep it safe, and away from people," said Minerva. "And make sure that continues after I die, in perpetuity."

"And that is well and good," said Annie. "But how can I trust you? I just met you. You seem like you're telling the truth, you do, but—"

"You don't have to give it to me," said Minerva. "I can't compel you. But I would take it."

Annie sighed. Her heart desperately wanted to give it away. To never see it again. But her thoughts went to Gabby, to the bookstore. The money. It would solve a lot of problems.

You'd be sowing more death into the world.

"Does anyone else know that you have it?" asked Minerva.

"My friend's wife," said Annie. "And one very interested buyer. He made an offer. A very generous one."

"Don't accept it," said Minerva. "No matter the price."

"It's easy to say that," said Annie. "But the money would

change our lives. It would make everything so much easier."

"I know," said Minerva. "The temptation is there. And I can't force you to do anything. But I will remain here, if you wish to give up the book. I will keep it secure."

Annie's heart screamed. "I need to think about it."

Minerva only nodded. The sadness in her face was there again, on the surface. "If you have any other questions for me, please, reach out." Minerva wrote down her phone number on a piece of paper, and handed it over. Annie realized that Minerva was telling her time was up. Minerva grabbed her purse, holding it close. Then, she remembered.

"Earlier, you said it was easier for everything you have to be from Ikea. I meant to ask, what did you mean by that?"

Minerva smiled again, briefly. "I think people think about it more now, with the advent of streaming music and television. With flatscreens. With 'minimalism', you know. With the push to rid ourselves of physical objects, to lean down with fewer belongings."

"What does that have to do with Ikea?"

"Physical objects have power, Annie," said Minerva. "The six items, they only make it more clear, but even everyday furniture, or a vinyl record, or a bookshelf, or a lamp. An apron worn by your mother for a lifetime."

"You mean things with sentimental value?"

"Sometimes," said Minerva. "But it could be something macabre as well. Items that witnessed murder, or bore it out. You see it in how we value antiques or memorabilia. A jersey worn on the field, during an important sports game are typically the most expensive memorabilia you can find. Or real props from a movie. They all contain power. Do you understand?"

"Yes," said Annie. "I still don't—"

"I want you to think about it," said Minerva. "When you look around your home, or a friend's home. About the power you've imbued into the items around you. You'll realize there's a lot there, surrounding you."

"Yes, but they're not dangerous," said Annie. "Often times, they give me comfort."

"Oh, I'm not arguing against that," said Minerva. "But dealing with these six items made me think of the possibilities. Made me wonder how many of these items exist. Passed around in estate sales, or on eBay, at antique malls. And once I started thinking about it, I couldn't stop. And from then on, I only bought disposable furniture. Disposable everything. Things that are mass produced, cheap, breakable. When something wears out, I replace it. Because the chances of this chair from Ikea being an item of power is very small. I have no attachment to it. No one does. It's safe."

Annie stared. She had more questions, but none would shine any more light on the experience that had driven Minerva to this life.

Annie got up to go, Minerva leading her to the door.

"Are you sure you don't want to leave me the book?" she asked, a final time.

"Yes," said Annie. "For now, at least."

"Okay," said Minerva, opening the door for her. Annie stepped through, and walked back to her car, unsure of what to say. Minerva stopped her.

"Annie," she said. Annie turned. "I understand, if you don't trust it to my care. But please, if you don't, don't sell it. Don't read it. Don't let anyone else know it exists. Bury it deep. Bury it so deep, no one will find it."

15

Annie headed home.

She'd found answers. Between talking to Judy Sullivan and to Minerva, she had a picture of what the book was, where it came from, and if it killed Brad.

It was an incomplete picture, one she might never fully see, but it was enough.

Annie drove home, a full day's drive, and she let the radio play, but quietly. She had used it to drive away the silence and her thoughts the day prior, but now, she used the time to think. About what she'd learned.

And what she believed.

The book sat next to her, in her purse, wrapped in newsprint, hidden from the naked eye. Minerva had said it had a pull, a gravity of its own, and now, sitting still, letting herself breathe, and feel, she could sense it.

It was subtle, slow and ponderous tentacles reaching out from the book and snaking into her heart. But they weren't strong. It was a soft tug. Annie imagined the pull could be stronger if the book wanted.

If the book wanted.

Minerva had described the book as alive, and Annie had to acknowledge it was somehow true. She felt it there, and had always felt it. Even when she was scanning the books they'd bought, and it sat there, unassuming at the time, she had noticed something from it.

What else did she believe?

Minerva had told her so much, and as she drove, she rolled it all over in her head. The six men, and their cursed six items. All of them dead by their hubris. Using a ritual to summon a power wed between the old and new.

The book itself, with the capability to transport you to the world inside it. Or to transform our world into it. And then to kill.

Or to grant your heart's desire.

Mike Sullivan had read the book searching for that granted wish, and it had killed him. How many had opened the book with that in mind? To find the true ending, the one that fulfilled your deepest wish? And how many had blundered into it, unknowingly?

Annie didn't know, and the dead were still dead despite their intent.

She believed the book was alive, and that it could kill. That it had killed Brad. She believed what Judy and Minerva had told her. She believed it in the abstract, the same way that she believed in the gravitational forces that create dead stars and black holes. Annie knew they existed and believed in them—but they were distant.

She had never encountered them, and if she did—they would rip her apart.

The book sat only a few feet away, and until she opened it, and delved inside—she didn't think she could truly believe.

Thinking yourself in circles, Annie. None of that matters, and you know it. What will you do with the book?

Ay, there's the rub. The book had killed Brad, and would kill again, if it was sold to Ted Montour, who would pass it on to his buyer. They might read it, they might not, but it would be in general circulation, to be passed on again and again, and kill along the way.

Keeping it to the simple facts made it easier for Annie to contain in her mind. The book had killed Brad. It would kill again, eventually, if let loose, even into a private collection.

Annie could give the book back to Minerva, for safekeeping, along with the other two cursed items she said she had.

Annie could sell the book to Ted, and forget about it. Take the money and run.

Annie could bury the book deep, where no one could find it.

What would Brad do, knowing what she knew?

He wouldn't sell it. That fact was firm in her mind. Despite Brad's capitalist tendencies, he was a kind and gentle man. He wouldn't propagate death if he could help it.

She could give it to Minerva. But there was something inside her, something that didn't trust Minerva. Not that she was lying. But Minerva wouldn't tell her where the book was kept, Annie was almost sure of it. And that didn't sit right with Annie. She wanted to *know* it was locked away, buried, isolated, and would never be found.

And Brad would have felt the same way.

And like a deadbolt sliding into place, it clicked shut in her mind. She would bury the book deep, hide it away somewhere where no one would find it, not ever, not even her.

It's not up to only you.

Brad's death hadn't affected only her, and Gabby was part owner of the book. And Gabby deserved to know the truth, and its part in Brad's death.

And a part in deciding what to do with it.

Annie wanted to be selfish, and self-righteous, and decide her own judgment, but Gabby had an equal say, just like her.

Would Gabby believe what Annie had found? The pull of that money would tempt a widow, who now would have to raise a child on a single income, regardless of the death attached to the book. And the story, at face value, was outlandish. It had taken hours and hours of time with the book, and talking to Judy and Minerva for Annie to be convinced, and even then, in the abstract.

Would Gabby believe?

Annie would make her believe.

*

Brad's car still sat parked in the driveway, and seeing it made Annie remember of the countless times she had pulled up to the house, to see the both of them, and then the three of them, after Buddy had been born. The car was a marker for Brad being there, right inside the door.

But he wasn't. And the realization pulled open a hollow wound inside Annie that had scarce time to heal.

Annie remembered Minerva's words. About objects, and the power they had.

She went up to the door and knocked. Gabby answered quickly, a sad smile on her face as she saw Annie. Gabby embraced her, squeezing her tightly as she entered. There was a distant shuffling, and then Buddy rounded a corner, and came in and joined the group hug.

"Hi, Buddy," said Annie.

"Aunt Annie, Aunt Annie," he said, into her thigh. He let go, and then Gabby let go as well, and they went into the living room. Buddy scattered back to his playroom, zooming around another corner.

They sat down, toys scattered around the floor, the television off. Buddy's noise echoed to them. Annie sat her purse on the coffee table in front of her. She felt the book inside. She had considered leaving it home, but it was right to have it there.

"How are you?" asked Annie.

"Bad," said Gabby, smiling, her eyes not smiling with her mouth. "But surviving."

Annie took a breath, looking at her friend. "And Buddy?"

"He's okay," said Gabby. "He's sad from time to time, but he's still young. I don't think he understands completely. His dad being gone—it's still a temporary thing. Eventually he'll realize—that—that he's not coming back." She took a deep breath. "We'll talk about it then."

Buddy's footsteps grew loud again, and he ran into the room.

"No running, honey," said Gabby, and Buddy slowed to

a fast walk and came to a screeching halt in front of Annie. He hugged her again, and then looked up at her, smiling.

"This is for you," he said, and handed over a picture he'd drawn in crayon. Annie took it and looked. An out-sized yellow sun shone down on stick figures in the middle of flowers.

"Oh, thank you," said Annie. "Who's in it?"

"This is all of us," said Buddy. "Mom and Dad and you, and me!" He pointed at himself last. "It's when we were at the playground together."

Annie forced herself not to cry, the memory refreshed. She held back tears, and instead just hugged Buddy again, holding him until her voice returned. "Oh, thank you, honey, it's very nice."

"You're welcome!" he yelled, and then wheeled away.

"Like I said," said Gabby. She smiled again. Annie took the picture and placed it underneath her purse so it wouldn't get lost. Gabby looked at her.

"You're back," said Gabby.

"I am," said Annie. She took a deep breath.

"You found something."

"I did," said Annie. "I found a lot. Not everything, but enough for a half-finished picture." Annie paused. Where to start? She stared at her purse, feeling the book inside.

"Well?"

"I'm sorry," said Annie. "It's going to sound crazy. But I'm going to tell you it all, even if it is." And she did, explaining everything she had seen and heard, about talking to Judy, and Minerva, and the pull of the book, and the six men and their six items, and their six deaths.

Gabby sat silently and listened, without interruption.

Annie started slowly, unsure of what to say, in what order, but soon the words spilled out of her. Soon they were all gone, and the room was quiet, as Gabby sat with everything Annie had said.

Gabby took a deep breath.

"You were right," she said. "It is crazy."

"I told you," said Annie. "But no one lied to me."

"I believe that."

"But do you believe me?"

Gabby looked at her, her eyes still sad, not saying anything.

"What do you think we should do?" asked Gabby, avoiding the answer.

"There's an abandoned well in a small park near the bookstore. The city is scheduled to fill it with concrete within the next two weeks. It's thirty feet deep. I want to drop the book down the hole, and let it get covered. It will never be discovered, never dug up. Buried forever."

Gabby said nothing, breathing deeply through her nose. "How much did Ted Montour offer for it?"

"100K."

"One hundred thousand dollars," said Gabby. "Buried in thirty feet of concrete."

"It kills people, Gabby."

"I—" she started, and exhaled. "I have a hard time believing that."

"Then how did Brad die?"

"Some madman," said Gabby. "Who's obsessed with the book."

"Who left no evidence," said Annie. "Who left no evidence with the other deaths. Who left the book in Brad's hands."

Gabby stared at Annie. "That money—it's not—" And Gabby stopped, and cried, tears running down her face, and she collapsed in her seat, sobbing. Annie went to her, and held her, as she bawled and bawled. It felt like infinity, time slowed to a crawl by sorrow.

Gabby stopped, eventually, all her tears gone.

"I need a tissue," she said, and got up, walking over to a bookshelf and grabbing a tissue, blowing her nose, and then doing it again with a second one. "I'm sorry, I just—"

"No, it's okay," said Annie. "I shouldn't have—"

Gabby threw the tissues away in the kitchen trash can and then went to the patio door. "I need fresh air." She went outside and Annie followed. They walked out into the chill afternoon, looking out on Gabby's property, leaning on the rail.

"I'm no better than Buddy," said Gabby, finally.

"What does that mean?"

"Brad's not coming back," said Gabby. "I keep expecting—I keep expecting him to walk through the door, and hug us both, and pick up Buddy, and spin him around, like he did every day when he came home."

"Gabby—"

"But he's not coming back," said Gabby. "I'm alone in this. And the idea terrifies me. Raising Buddy without help, with no one to ease the burden—I can't handle it."

"You're not alone," said Annie. "I'm here. And Brad's parents. And so many more. We'll all help. We will find a way through. We all love you, and Buddy. We'll make it."

Gabby stood silently. "And the thought of that money." She took a breath. "It wouldn't solve everything. It's not enough for that, not forever. But it's enough to give me some breathing room. Properly invested, maybe it *could* be enough." She sighed again. "And yes, it seems too much of a coincidence for the book to be involved with so many deaths. But what if it's not? What if we're dumping it down a hole for no reason at all?"

Annie stood silently next to her. The wind cut through them, and she shivered. It felt familiar, this feeling. Of standing next to Gabby, quietly, in the cold. Just long enough—

Deja vu, again.

But that was impossible. Annie shook the thought away.

"We don't have to stand out here," said Gabby. "I feel better."

"No, wait," said Annie. "You don't have to believe in the power of the book to kill, or grant wishes. You just have to believe me." Annie took a breath. "I tried to think of what Brad would do, if faced with the same choice. If he believed, as I do, that the book kills whoever opens it. What would he do?"

"He would bury it," said Gabby. "He wouldn't doubt his decision, either. He'd figure out a plan, and execute."

Annie met her eyes. "That's exactly what I thought." She paused. "You knew him better than anyone. He wouldn't take a chance, not with something he knew was dangerous. He'd get rid of it."

Gabby took another deep breath. "You're right, Annie. You're right." Annie hugged her.

"We'll get through this, together," she said, softly.

"We will," said Gabby. They went back inside, into the pleasant warmth of the house. Buddy's noise could still be heard from his playroom.

"Do you have it?" asked Gabby.

"Yes, in my purse."

"Will you take care of it?"

"Of course," said Annie. "I'll do it today." Annie picked up her purse and grabbed the picture Buddy had given her.

"Will you come back, after?" asked Gabby. "We can put on a movie, or something—"

"Of course," said Annie. "I'll be back in a few hours."

Buddy scampered into the room again. "Mom, can I go play outside?"

"You promise not to go past your clubhouse?" asked Gabby.

"I promise," said Buddy.

"Say goodbye to Aunt Annie, and once she's gone, we'll get you dressed, okay?"

"Okay," said Buddy. He hugged Annie. "Bye Aunt Annie, love youuu."

"Love you too, Buddy," said Annie, hugging him. Gabby walked her to the door.

"Love you," said Gabby, quietly.

"Love you too," said Annie, and then she walked to her car, past Brad's van.

Annie drove to the bookstore, devoid of the anxiety and worry that had lived with her since the book had entered her life. She would drop it down that well, and it would be gone forever. She stopped at the bookstore, but didn't go inside, instead walking down the block to the small park.

It was nice, quiet, only used by the neighborhood, with a playground and a small field, where the kids played soccer or football. The well stood adjacent, and had stood there, capped for decades, a relic to the time when someone lived on the land. It hadn't been used in over a hundred years, and after a couple of kids had a close call, after they had pried the cap off, the city had decided to fill it with concrete.

Annie pushed the cap aside, and looked down, the bottom not visible. No one would go down there in the two weeks before it was filled, and afterwards, no one would find it. Not ever.

Annie took a deep breath, and propped her purse on the other side of the cap, and pulled the book out, still wrapped in newsprint. The paper was a little askew, and she pulled it off.

Oh no. No no no.

The book was gone.

Well, not gone.

Replaced.

In its stead was a children's book, slim, of similar size, but for a younger age.

Buddy.

16

Buddy ran across his backyard, stomping through the dead grass of early winter. He couldn't see his playhouse, not yet, but he would soon.

He breathed hard, his breath fogging in front of him. He looked back to the house one time, to see if Mom was watching him. She wasn't outside, and he didn't see her face at the glass of the patio door.

It was okay. He was okay alone.

Mom was sad, and he had tried to cheer her up, but it didn't seem to help. She was still sad.

But Buddy had a plan. He would cheer her up. He knew exactly what would do it.

He ran through the small gate in their back fence, and the door clacked as it swung shut behind him. He could see his clubhouse now. It stood inside a group of trees, hidden away. He had picked that spot for that very reason.

Mom and Dad had wanted his clubhouse to be in the backyard, but their backyard didn't have any trees in it, and just behind their backyard were the woods, and that's where he wanted it.

No one's clubhouse was out in the open. It was too dangerous. Here, he would be hidden from monsters and bad guys. It had taken a while, but Mom and Dad had finally agreed, and they all built the clubhouse together, putting it right in the middle of a group of trees, so the bad guys couldn't find it.

Buddy ran down the path that led to his clubhouse. He ducked under a handful of branches, and went inside, hidden by the dead leaves stuck to the outside.

The inside was small, but had enough room for Buddy, as he sat down in his chair in the corner, next to his table. It had some stuff already on it—an old comic book given to him by his Dad, a handful of specially chosen sticks and rocks, and a few action figures, some missing arms, legs, or heads.

Buddy was going to make his mom less sad. He unzipped his jacket, despite the cold, and emptied his pockets. Out came a pile of things, with glue, tape, a pair of scissors, and a box of crayons.

Mom said Dad was gone, but Buddy would make sure that Dad would never be gone. He'd make a di-o-rama like he did in daycare, but in this one, it would be him, and Mom, and Dad, and Mom could look at it whenever she got sad.

Buddy got to work. He had stolen a shoebox from Mom and Dad's closet, and in it he started putting together the rocks and sticks, using glue to stick things together as he worked. His small fingers twisted the sticks, pushing them together, adding glue to the stones, until they formed the shapes he wanted. First him, then Mom, and finally Dad.

With all of them roughly formed, Buddy stopped to look at his work. He wanted to add small things with them, and then add color with his crayons.

But he'd been working at it for a while, and he could hear his Dad in his head. It was something he'd been practicing.

Buddy missed Dad.

Mom had sat him down, and talked him through what had happened. That Dad had died, and wouldn't be around anymore. That he should take the memories he had with him, and cherish them. That was the word his mom used, and she had told him what it meant.

To hold on to them.

Buddy had listened and nodded, but he didn't really understand everything his mom had told him. But she seemed sad, and he didn't want to upset her, so he had agreed, and hugged her. It seemed to make things better, so that's what he did.

It was hard for him to hold on to memories, like she had said. There were a few that really stuck out, but most were already gone, long before Dad had died.

But Buddy *could* hold on to his Dad's voice. That was easy. It was loud and clear in his head, whenever he thought about it. He could summon it without effort, and he did now.

That's enough, Buddy. You've been working pretty hard. How about a reading break?

It was something Buddy remembered happening his

whole life. They would do something for a while, and when it was time for a break, it was a chance to read. At first, Mom or Dad would read to him, but as soon as he was able, he would read to himself, with either of his parents reading their own book next to him.

It felt normal to Buddy, to read a book while you took a break, and he figured it was another way to remember his dad. When he would read, he could picture him sitting nearby, reading his own grown-up book.

Buddy reached into the inside pocket of his jacket, where he had put the book he had traded with Aunt Annie. He had watched his parents do it at the little library down the street. They had taken a book and put one of their own back, so it was okay for him to do the same. He had given Aunt Annie his favorite book, too, and he hoped she would like it. She loved books, he knew that, just like Dad did.

Buddy didn't know this book, but the cover was scary, with two scary kids on it, and it said *Choose Your Fate* which Buddy could read, but didn't know what fate was. But he understood most of the rest of the title *The Mystery of the Sentinel Lodge.* He had other books that said the word mystery, and he really liked them. They were like puzzles, and he and Dad would always try to work out the answer before the end of the book.

He could do that with this one, he'd bet. He was smart.

Buddy opened the book and read.

Your breath catches in your lungs as the chill air enters them. You stand outside of the Sentinel Lodge, six stories tall, staring down at you. The Rockies surround you, mountains towering high.

A voice startles you.

"You must be my new assistant caretaker," said the voice, and you turn to see a man who looks to be in his 50s, with graying hair and cold eyes. They are squinted against the glare of the sun off the snowpack.

"I am," you say.

"I'm Carl Douglas," he says, and he extends a hand. You reach out and shake it, his hand big, enveloping yours, and he smiles as he squeezes.

"Nice to meet you," he said. "Follow me inside."

TURN TO PAGE 3

Buddy struggled with some of the words, but he was smart, and he used clues to piece together what they meant, or at least probably what they meant. But he was also excited. This book was different than anything he'd read before. As he read, it was like he was in the story. He turned to page three, and the story continued. At the bottom of the next page, he got a choice! He'd never gotten to choose how the story went, and he chose to explore the halls. From what Buddy had read, adventures never happened if you stayed in your room. You had to go find it.

Buddy didn't realize the world was changing around him, his nose deep in the book. The words he didn't know didn't matter, he pushed through, reading as fast as he could. He followed his path in his mind, through the book. He decided to leave his room in the middle of the night, going left down the hall, and then went upstairs. Buddy flipped through the pages, reading quickly. He could feel his heart beat hard in his chest. He *needed* to know how his adventure would end.

He flipped the page, and in the book, he came face to face with the twins on the front cover, and as he pored over the page, they took his character's hands, and they pulled him into a room nearby, and then he saw the big bold letters—

THE END

What? No, that wasn't fair. He was just getting into the adventure, and Buddy was convinced he'd solve the mystery of the hotel. He'd go back, he'd find the right path—

But the book was closed. He didn't remember closing it, and try as he might, it wouldn't open again. He yanked at the paper, but it stayed shut, no matter how hard his small hands pulled.

He sighed, and went to put down the book, and get back to the diorama, but then he realized it was all gone, and he wasn't in his clubhouse anymore.

Buddy sat on a bed. His feet dangled off the edge, the room dark. It smelled musty and faintly of smoke.

Where was he?

There was a thumping noise outside his door, and Buddy realized it was footsteps, as they walked away. It sounded like his dad, who would walk by Buddy's bedroom door during the night. He hadn't thought Buddy would be awake, but sometimes he was, reading beneath the covers, with a flashlight.

But whoever that was, it wasn't Dad. The book was still in his hand, and he looked down, and realized.

I'm in the Sentinel Lodge.

Buddy felt a nervousness enter his stomach, and the back of his knees ached with a sharp suddenness. His clubhouse felt a million miles away, and the safety and closeness of his home, and his mom, felt even further.

His clubhouse was safe.

Buddy knew the lodge was not safe. He felt it, sitting there, even for a moment. He was young, yes, but his parents had coached him early on, that when a situation felt wrong, it meant *it was* wrong. Trust yourself, they had said.

He desperately, desperately wanted to go home.

The room felt unsafe, he knew that much. And whatever stomped outside his door was a bad guy. He was sure of that as well. He would bet there were a lot of bad guys here. Buddy needed to go home, and if he wanted to do that, he would have to leave the lodge.

He had a plan in mind. Buddy would leave this place. He would find his way home, to his mom, and to the memories of his dad.

Buddy hopped off the bed, the carpet padding the small sound of him landing. He crept to the door, pressing his ear to the wood, listening for that thumping noise, knowing it was a bad man. He'd have to get past him, he knew, if he wanted to escape.

He reached up and opened the door, creaking open, and he walked out into a hallway, the patterned carpet making it seem infinite. He looked left and right, and the left was shorter to the staircase, and he went that way, hurrying, not quite running, not yet.

A door creaked open to his right, and Buddy froze, not knowing what else to do. Darkness lay inside, and he stopped, and slowly craned his neck, staring into it. Twin shapes emerged, walking in step. The twins from the cover of the book. He looked down, and they matched perfectly.

They reached the entrance of the door and extended their hands in tandem.

"We want to play," they said, together.

Buddy ran then, down the hall, toward the stairs, and scampered down them as fast as he could. His stomach ached, and a sour taste filled his whole mouth, but he wouldn't stop to throw up, he needed to get out of the lodge, had to escape.

Buddy hit the stairs fast, and climbed down, as quickly as he could, down a flight, two flights, three flights, four flights, and then he was on the first floor. He had been in a hotel before, and knew what a lobby looked like, and he had to walk through, and there would be big doors at the front, and he would walk outside, and find his house. It would be out there, somewhere. It had to be.

Buddy ran, barely seeing the chairs, the wall paneling, the lodge that was multiple times over removed from time, the dissonant placement of the windows and decorations. He only ran for where he knew the front door must be.

"Checking out, sir?" asked a voice. It was thin and reedy, and Buddy froze out of surprise. The voice was calm, and Buddy turned to see him. A man stood behind the counter, wearing fancy clothes that Buddy didn't recognize. His hair was slicked back, and his eyes were sunken into his face, orbs peering out from deep in his skull. He was alive, but looked like he shouldn't be.

He stared at Buddy with those eyes, appraising him. The man stood behind the counter, waiting for Buddy.

Buddy stood there, his heart pounding, his lungs heaving. He forced words out.

"Yes. Checking out," he said. He knew what that meant.

He knew it meant he could leave, if he checked out.

"Can I have your name, and room key?" asked the man. "I can get you sorted right away."

"Buddy—I mean, William Winters," said Buddy. The man would want his full name, he knew. And for the key? He didn't have a key, in the book he was an assistant caretaker, he reached into his pockets, but there was nothing there. He only had the book.

Buddy walked slowly to the counter, looking up at him. The man's face stayed the same, only a small courteous smile. Buddy reached up and slid the book over to the man. Buddy stared at him, waiting.

"Excellent, sir, excellent." The man had a notebook out in front of him, and he scribbled a few notes.

"Alright, sir, you're good to go," said the man. "May I ask how your stay was?"

Buddy stared. He swallowed.

"Good," he said, his voice quiet.

"Excellent to hear," said the man. "I hope you come back."

"So I can go?" asked Buddy.

"Of course, of course," said the man. "Have a good night."

Buddy stared at him for a moment longer, and walked quickly to the front door.

"Oh excuse my manners," said the man, who hustled past Buddy, and opened the door for him. "Please."

Buddy stared up at him, and saying nothing more, walked outside the lodge. He stood in snow, ankle deep. It covered the parking lot, a rectangle of pavement in front of him, barely visible. The light from the lodge reached the edge of the parking lot, but beyond that, there was only a dim, gray glow.

There was one other source of light out in the snow. Dim lights shined on walls of green hedges. Buddy stared.

"It's a maze," said the man, from the open door. "I'd steer clear."

Buddy glanced back at him, and the door was already shut against the cold, the man disappearing back inside.

Buddy was suddenly freezing, and a wind blew through, and he couldn't breathe, and he zipped up his jacket, and pulled down the hood, and it helped a little. He walked.

He knew, knew somehow, that if he walked far enough, it would get him home. He just had to escape the cold. Buddy walked through the parking lot. The road was there, he knew it, and if he followed the road, it would take him to a city, which would lead to help. His parents had told him, if he was lost.

Find a place with people. Ask them to call your phone number.

Buddy knew the hotel was bad, filled with bad guys. He was past the parking lot, and he walked down what he thought was the road, but it was hard to see, surrounded by the white of the snow, and the darkness. He couldn't see very far, and the wind cut through him again, and he was cold, so cold. Buddy had never been this cold before, and his thighs ached, the cold settling into them. He wore a jacket, which helped keep his torso warmer, but only wore jeans on his legs, and he reached down to rub his thighs, trying to warm them.

The terrible pain in his stomach and knees was gone, that he was away from the lodge, but something else was settling into him, a deep sadness that he didn't have the word for. He walked and walked, and it seemed like he should have seen something by now.

He wanted his mom. He wanted his house. Where were they?

Buddy turned around, looking back. Could he still see the lodge?

He saw nothing but the gray dim surrounding him. The lodge was gone behind him.

He had to walk forward. He had to keep going. His house was up ahead, he knew it. Mom was up ahead. She would be there, and she would warm him up. He would drink a hot chocolate, and she would put a big marshmallow in it.

But it was cold, so cold. Buddy couldn't feel his fingers, stuffing them into his pockets, but it didn't help, there was only cold.

The cold had settled into Buddy. He just wanted to see his mom again.

He couldn't feel his feet, and he stumbled, and he fell.

He just wanted to see his mom again.

*

Gabby stirred the pasta, to make sure it didn't stick to the bottom. It still had ten more minutes in the water, but she hated having to scrape soggy pasta off the bottom of the pan.

Cooking dinner brought her comfort. It was consistent, necessary, and it helped care for herself and Buddy. It helped soothe all the parts of her that ached, the raw parts inside scraped clean by Brad's death.

Where was Buddy?

He had asked to go play in his clubhouse, and he took

crafting supplies, despite how he tried to hide it. He wanted to make something, which was pretty innocuous, but she had told him not to stay out too long, and Buddy was prone to getting too focused on a task, and losing sight of the outside world.

She went to the back patio door and looked out. She didn't see him, which meant he was still in his clubhouse.

The pasta had ten minutes, which was enough time to walk back there, grab him, and come back.

Gabby didn't bother grabbing her coat. It was cold outside, but she wouldn't be out long enough for it to matter. She marched across the backyard, and through the gate, into the forest property that sat behind their lot.

The clubhouse was immediately in view. Buddy always thought it was hidden, but it was very easy to spot, especially with adult eyes. But the illusion made him happy, so they had always played along.

Gabby walked and soon was close. She stood outside the small copse of trees where his clubhouse was.

"Buddy," she said. "It's time to call it a day. Dinner's almost ready. We should get you cleaned up before we eat."

There was no answer, and no sound.

"Buddy," she said. He'd hidden in there before, not wanting to leave. "Don't make me come in there after you."

Still nothing.

She sighed. "Buddy—" She wanted to threaten punishment, but after Brad's death, she hesitated to heap on any more negativity. But he was testing her.

She crouched, and pushed aside the low branches and leaves in the way, pushing her way to the clubhouse. She peeked into the open door.

No she said, all she could muster, a soft sound no one heard.

Buddy laid on the floor of the clubhouse, completely still. She rushed in, scraping her sides through the small doorway, and slowly flipped him over.

His eyes were shut, his skin pale, his lips blue.

She didn't understand, her hands going to his hands, over his chest, to his throat, to his face, checking for injury, checking for anything—

"Please, bubba, please, answer me," she said, but he said nothing. He was freezing cold, almost hurting her hands to touch him, it didn't make sense, didn't make sense, it wasn't that cold outside, not even below 50 degrees—

She squeezed his hands, hoping something would make him open his eyes, she couldn't bear this, and then she saw the book, tears welling in her eyes.

"No, that's impossible," she said, a whisper, tears streaming down her face. She pulled the book from his small hand, closed. *Choose Your Fate: The Mystery of the Sentinel Lodge.*

He had taken it from Annie. He had read it.

It had killed him.

A thousand emotions filled Gabby, her heart racing, her eyes choked with tears, the utter unfairness of it all overwhelming her. She stared at the book, hoping it would burn with all her will.

But then she stopped. She remembered Annie's words.

The book was a test. That's what she said. It had the power to kill, yes, but also, somewhere inside, was the key to your heart's greatest wish.

"Find your way through the book," said Gabby, quietly to herself. "Find your way to the true ending, and your heart's deepest wish will be granted."

She looked at Buddy, staring at his serene face. She kissed him on his cheeks, a soft kiss, her lips cold from it.

She would bring him back. Him and Brad both.

Gabby stared at the book, opened it, and read.

17

Annie sprayed the book with lighter fluid, in the small hole she'd dug in her backyard.

She had bought a full jug, and sprayed until the book was drowning. She poured herself a small trail, the fumes rising in a cloud of gas over the hole, and then lit it, the fire snaking away.

There was a BOOPH, and the puddle ignited, a wave of heat washing over Annie in the cold air. It was gone quickly, the cold overwhelming it, and soon the puddle of fluid was gone, the smoke rising into the air, dissipating, leaving only the book.

She approached, staring.

It still looked new, fresh off the printing press. The spine was hard and crisp, the pages cut perfectly. No weather, no wrinkles. It was as perfect as it ever would be.

Annie knew it would do nothing, but she had tried anyway. She had run the book over in her car, taken her chef's knife to it, had tried to destroy it in a dozen ways, but nothing hurt it. Nothing could damage it, or dampen it, or tear the pages.

Intrinsic.

That was the word Minerva had used. Destroying the book was as impossible as attacking gravity or time. Whatever power the book had been imbued with was fundamental, and could not be altered.

Annie stared, looking at the front cover for the hundredth time, just like Gabby had, like Buddy had, like every victim had, before they had opened it, and the book had killed them.

Annie only had snapshots in her mind of the past two weeks.

The mad drive back to Gabby's house.

The frantic run to Buddy's clubhouse.

Finding the bodies, next to each other.

The sorrow, the screams.

The police, the tragedy, the phone calls, the twin funeral.

Annie told the police the truth they would believe. That she had just come back from a trip, was visiting Gabby and Buddy, had gone out to run some errands, and when she came back to their house, they had been dead.

None of that was a lie. She didn't mention the book, taking it from Gabby's hands, one of which was bruised and bloody, fingers broken in multiple places.

She remembered screaming, she did, a hoarse horrible primal sound that had erupted from her. She didn't know how long she screamed, but her voice was gone by the time the police arrived, and she couldn't speak at the funeral. Annie sat in the back row, away from everything, watching as Gabby's family and the rest of her friends mourned the sudden loss of an entire household.

The family all comforted her. They knew how close she was to Gabby, to Buddy, to Brad. She had lost them, too.

And it *was* genuine. They did care for her.

But still, they suspected her of something. There was a great mystery hanging in the air. A whole family, dead, in just a few weeks. Both parents killed by brutal attacks, a child dead from exposure, with no apparent cause or suspects. No evidence, no leads. A happy family, that loved each other, with no enemies.

All dead.

Annie knew the truth, the truth that her feelings of paranoia, of anxiety and worry, everyone at the funeral, at the wake, they all eyed her, stared at her, whispered under their breath about her involvement—all of it because she had lied about the book.

She knew the truth.

And she felt guilty.

She was aware of the cognitive dissonance, of the two warring thoughts inside her mind, but she couldn't dismiss either, and so she felt both guilt and rage, unending, fiery rage, directed at the cursed book.

The rage led to the burning, the cutting, the myriad attempts at crushing, destroying, *obliterating* the book.

Annie remembered her doubt. Even after convincing Gabby that the book had killed Brad, Annie still had doubts herself. She hadn't seen the book in action, and hadn't read it. She'd only heard the accounts of Judy Sullivan, of Minerva. Minerva had told her the book was alive, was sentient, and influenced the world for outcomes it desired.

She had believed it was alive. But she had thought of it the way a plant was alive. Sure, it lived. It needed sun and water to survive, and maybe its leaves were poisonous, after thousands of years of evolution, to keep the animals at bay. But it couldn't talk or affect the world meaningfully.

But she believed it all now. The book *was* alive, and not like a plant, but more like an insidious predator, waiting to strike, an immortal creature trapped in an innocent form.

Because she *knew* it had spoken to Buddy. It had whispered in his ear, had used its influence to pull him over to her purse in the few short minutes the two of them were outside, and convinced Buddy to take that book, and replace it with one of his own.

Did Buddy even realize? No, just like she didn't realize it while it was happening. Ever since first laying eyes on it, the book had been on her mind. From when she opened her eyes in the morning to when she went to sleep, the book was always there. It pulled at her, all the time, always reminding her of its presence, and pulling her to open it, and read it.

But it had recognized the danger. It knew that she was planning on burying it, and it had taken drastic action.

Annie removed the book from the hole, and carried it, putting it back in her purse, back where it had been, the weight carried by her.

She looked around her small house. It was a mess. She hadn't cleaned or tidied in weeks, ever since they'd found the book, and there was nothing in her. She was hollow, paper thin, and a light touch would break through.

In the days after Gabby and Buddy's deaths, Annie had walked, unable to sit still, unable to focus on a book, or television. So she walked, without destination or direction. Her feet ached after a week of this, but the pain was a welcome distraction.

But even that brought no solace now. The book had recaptured her mind. With two more on its tally, it aimed its sights at her again.

The book wanted her to stay here, to wallow in misery.

Annie instead put on her shoes, grabbed her purse, and went to the bookstore.

*

She hadn't opened the bookstore since before Brad's death, and it was as she left it. The books in their shelves, the silence of the store, the pleasant must of the old paper. The occasional drone of a car driving by on the road outside. Dust hung in the air as she opened the door.

She closed it behind her, drifting through the store.

It felt alien and like home, a familiar and safe place now tied inextricably to the anchor in her purse. Why had she come here?

Comfort, Annie. Books have always been your comfort.

It was true, she had always retreated to an open book when the world had overwhelmed her. But it wasn't the only reason she had come here.

She still needed to decide about the book.

They had been dead set on burying the book deep, covered by thirty feet of concrete.

But the book had adjusted, and avoided the burial, claiming two more innocents in the process. The concrete had been poured in the meantime.

It changed nothing. There were other places she could put the book, that were out of reach of anyone else, for as long as humans existed.

Her choices were the same. Bury it, give it to Minerva, or sell the book to Ted.

Ted had called a few times since they'd spoken at Brad's funeral. Annie hadn't answered, and Ted's voicemails had told her his buyer was still interested, and had been quite insistent on getting his hands on the book. Maybe even offering to up the price if it wasn't high enough.

But Annie hadn't answered, and hadn't called him back. What would she tell him? She couldn't accept the blood money now, no matter the amount.

Then why haven't you buried it?

And the same cognitive dissonance was there, that both blamed herself and raged against the book, because she knew why. She knew why she hadn't found a new permanent place for the book, far away from prying eyes.

Because her choices *weren't* the same. There was a fourth option, and there always had been. But it was one she had never acknowledged.

It was to read the book, and find the way through, and wish her friends back to life.

The thought was stupid. Every single person who'd read the book had died. All of them. The book was a trap, a vicious cycle once you knew the truth, of thinking the only way to undo the horror it caused was to open it yourself, all the while only insuring you would propagate death.

It was attractive all the same, the idea that all of it could be undone. That if you solved the simple puzzle of the book, all this pain and trauma could be erased.

It knows its power, and uses it to kill.

She was at an impasse, and she had come to the store to help her think. Being surrounded by those books, by the power of their words, it would clarify her thoughts. It would push back on her grief, long enough for her to decide. A good decision.

But another thought lingered there. The last time she had decided to bury the book forever, it had used its power to kill two more, pulling Buddy and Gabby into its orbit and murdering them.

Would it cause more bloodshed, if she attempted to bury it once more?

It was the right thing to do, but could she bear the cost?

She stared at the book, bare, out on the counter. Was it influencing her now? How much power did it have? Annie worried that if had that much power—

A knock on the door and she jumped. The store was closed, and she wasn't expecting any visitors. Truthfully, she wanted to be alone. She stood still, hoping they would leave.

A few moments passed, and then the door shook with three loud raps.

Annie sighed, putting the book under the counter, out of sight, and going to the door. She peered out the glass and saw a thin, well-dressed woman standing there, staring right back at her.

"We're closed," she said, through the glass. "Sorry."

"Please, Ms. Maddox," she said. "I need to talk to you."

She knows my name?

Annie stared for a moment and then ducked away. "Please, I don't know when we'll re-open. Please call before you visit."

"Ms. Maddox, I have tried to contact you multiple times, but all attempts have failed. I have not come all this way to be turned away. Please, let me in. I need to talk to you about the book."

Annie's stomach ached, and she realized she recognized this woman. The woman from the auction, who had tried to outbid Fleming, but had failed.

"W—what book?" Annie asked.

"*The Mystery of the Sentinel Lodge*."

Annie paused for a moment longer, taking a deep breath. "What do you know about it?"

"I know a lot," said the woman. "I know it's powerful. I know it can kill. And I know how to read it, and come away with your heart's greatest wish."

Annie's heart beat even harder in her chest. Could she trust her? She took a deep breath, and unlocked the door. She opened it. The woman extended a slim hand, and matched it with a similar smile.

"Alex Watson," she said. "Pleased to make your acquaintance."

18

“You were at the auction.”

“You noticed,” said Alex, as she perused the shelves of The Book Barn.

“You and Andrew Fleming had quite the bidding war,” Annie said, walking around to the other narrow walkway, moving past her, back to the counter, and behind it. She felt safer there. Annie eyed the book and pushed it farther back under the counter, behind other clutter. Alex was still looking at the stacks of paperbacks, as if she was just another customer.

“Yes,” said Alex. “We did.” She paused, grabbing a paperback off the shelf and staring at the cover before replacing it. “He stole it from you, didn’t he?”

Annie stared at her.

"How do you know that?"

"I've pieced it together," said Alex. "Given who was at the auction. If Fleming had bought the book originally, you never would have had it. You don't know Fleming, and you and your late partner don't seem the type to hunt people down for a single book. So, you had the book, and Fleming realized it. And if he had bought it from you, you wouldn't have gone and gotten it back. And this is presumably before you truly realized what you had."

"We didn't really know," said Annie. "I suspected something, but—"

"But you dismissed it. Because of course you would. It's crazy. A book can't kill someone," said Alex, walking closer to the counter.

Annie didn't respond. What was her game?

Silence hung between them, as Alex glanced at her, and then back at the books.

"I wanted to apologize," Alex said, finally.

"For what?"

"I feel responsible for all of this."

"What do you mean?"

"I should have scouted better," said Alex. "I made an assumption, the same assumption as Fleming. I could have scouted better, knew which lot the book was in, and could have headed all of this off at the pass. It would have avoided a lot of bloodshed. A lot of heartache."

"I appreciate it," said Annie, "but it's not your fault. You couldn't have known."

"But I did know," said Alex. She took a breath. "I did know, and should have known better." She paused. "It's here, isn't it?"

Annie didn't need to clarify what Alex meant. She meant the book. She didn't answer, not wanting to admit the truth, and not wanting to lie, knowing Alex would see right through it. But Annie knew it didn't matter, because the silence gave Alex the answer, regardless.

"It's okay," she said. "I'm not going to take it from you, like Fleming. I only want to talk."

Annie considered her words.

"How did you know it's here?" Annie asked.

"I can feel it," said Alex. "I would say it's a sixth sense, but I don't appreciate that idiom. We have many senses, and the book, and objects like it, pull on strings connected to some part of us we have no name for. Most people only recognize the feeling as nerves, or some instinct they have no handle on. But I can feel it when I'm nearby."

Annie considered her. She remained calm, even while describing this. They had spoken *around* the topic of the book, subtly acknowledging its power, and its danger, but still, she knew nothing about Alex, or why she was here.

"You said you wanted to talk," said Annie. "What do you want to talk about?"

"The book," said Alex, letting herself a slim smile, before it disappeared again. "The book, and what to do with it."

"That's all well and good, Alex, but I don't know you. You're a stranger I saw from afar at an auction. You clearly know about the book, and have done a lot of digging if you do indeed know all of it, and aren't bullshitting. And I know I let you in the door, but who are you? Aside from someone with a spare twenty grand lying around to buy rare books?"

Alex looked at her now, Alex's face still calm. Annie briefly wondered if there was any anger in her at all.

"That's a fair request," she said. "Who am I? I'm a collector, I suppose, but not in the same way Andrew Fleming was. I'm also a dealer of sorts."

"You collect books?"

"Well, in this case, yes, but no, not exclusively books. I collect artifacts like the book you have. Things with power. Sometimes innocuous, sometimes not."

"Isn't that dangerous?"

"It can be," said Alex. "But I only collect them. I don't use them. Not ever. You've spoken to Minerva, I assume?"

"Yes," said Annie. "You know her?"

"We've been in contact once or twice. I'm not too different from her, in a way. Can I ask you a question?"

"You've already asked me a handful of them," said Annie. "What's one more?"

"Why didn't you leave the book with Minerva? I know she gave you the option."

"I didn't trust her," said Annie. "I don't know why."

Alex stood silent for a moment. "Can I posit a theory and see if it agrees with you?"

"Go for it."

"Do you know anyone that collects war memorabilia? Military historians?"

"No," said Annie. "I don't really see the appeal."

"I understand it on an abstract level, holding something of historical value. Wars, distasteful and bloody as they are, are of incredible historical value. They shape the world, and having something from a war or battle means you hold something that *helped* shape the world. But problems arise when you meet these people, in real life, at conventions or one-on-one, and you realize it goes beyond that for many of them. Many of them fetishize the bombs, the helmets, the guns, the bayonets, some of them even searching out weapons or items associated with high kill counts. Not all, but the handful I've met made me dislike the whole. But regardless of the ethical quandaries surrounding collecting weapons of death, it *is* almost universally agreed upon that all such weapons be disarmed prior to sale. Bombs or grenades are disarmed. Guns may still be fired, but are largely kept out of use. They become historical artifacts. Are you following me?"

"I think so," said Annie. "Are you saying I didn't trust Minerva because she didn't disarm the artifacts?"

"Yes," said Alex. "And some of the meaning gets lost in the metaphor. But it is true, she doesn't disarm them. She merely hides them. Under lock and key, somewhere only she knows. And having spoken to her, I believe it is with the best of intentions. She's been personally affected by the items, and believes the best thing to do is bury them. But I also believe that your feelings were correct."

"You think it's dangerous to bury them?"

"Yes," said Alex. "Would you bury a live, unexploded bomb?"

"No."

"Then why is this different?" asked Alex. "In all honesty, it's more dangerous than a bomb. The bomb goes off once. These items are infinite, if not taken care of properly. They want to be used. And maybe Minerva will keep them contained and she won't give in, or someone else won't find them. But my bet is that eventually something bad will happen, and we'll see them in the wild again."

Annie considered Alex's words. "Why are you different,

then?"

"Because I disarm them," said Alex. "I don't keep anything that isn't powerless, and I certainly don't sell anything that still has its power."

"You *disarm* them?" asked Annie. "How the hell do you do that?"

"It varies," said Alex. "Sometimes it's simple. Sometimes—sometimes it's dangerous."

"How many of these items do you have now?"

"A few dozen."

"A few *dozen*?" asked Annie. Her mind boggled at dealing with dozens of things like the book, that with one single mistake, could quickly kill a handful of people.

"Yes," said Alex. "This is over years, of course. And some items are quite innocuous. Not dangerous whatsoever, even when they had their powers."

"How long have you been following the book?"

"People in my circle have been aware of it for quite some time."

"Your circle?" asked Annie. "There are others like you?"

"Not exactly like me," said Alex. "Most people only dabble. Few do it full time, like I do. But yes, I keep in touch with a handful of others. We keep each other informed. It's in everyone's best interests."

"How long, then?"

"Years," said Alex. "But just because we're aware of it doesn't mean it's within reach. The book doesn't want to be captured by someone who knows what it is, without intention of reading it. It wants to float along, be read, cause chaos, and move on to another unknowing owner."

"You act like you know it."

Alex paused, thinking. "Once you've handled enough of these items, particularly the dangerous ones, you get an idea of how they operate. And they are alive, to some extent. Imbued with the power of a god or a curse, or some other awful thing. It never turns out well. It always ends in death."

Annie stared at her. "Where does your money come from?"

"From dealing in these items," said Alex. "Even the disarmed objects can be sold for quite a pretty penny. I used to have my family's money at my disposal. But after some unpleasantness, I'm on my own. I still do fine."

"You want to disarm the book?" asked Annie. "Take away its power?"

"Yes."

"And what if you can't?"

"We cross that bridge when we come to it," said Alex. "But I haven't failed yet."

Annie took a breath, and pulled the book out from under the counter, and put it on top, in full view. Alex stopped, and looked at it.

"Powerful," said Alex. "I can feel it even more, now."

"It wants you to read it?"

"Of course," said Alex. "It's what it exists to do. That is its purpose."

Annie nodded. "So, how do we disarm it?"

Alex sighed. "Most likely, we'll have to give it what it wants."

"What does that mean?"

"We have to read it," said Alex. "Well, one of us does."

19

"It kills people," said Annie. "That's all it does. And the only way we can disarm is to read it, and do what, exactly?"

"Get the true ending, I believe," said Alex. "It says it right there, on the book. It asks, 'Can you solve the mystery of the Sentinel Lodge?' and I believe that is the key. Solve the mystery, and defeat the book. Get your wish."

"Mike Sullivan himself couldn't solve it, and he wrote the damn thing, Alex. It kills *everyone* who reads it. It's all well and good to believe that we can read the book, and solve all our problems, but it just looks like a suicide mission, and despite everything, I do not want to die in the grasp of some cursed book!"

Annie had raised her voice, nearly shouting. Her heart thumped in her chest, her breath coming hard. She hadn't meant to yell, but Alex was so damn calm, and her friends were dead, dead and they weren't ever coming back—

"First, Mike Sullivan underestimated the book. It's clear at this point that it is formidable, and most likely reshapes itself between readings." Alex paused. "And it doesn't kill *everyone* who reads it."

Annie stared at her. "Mike Sullivan, dead. The man I bought it from, dead. Fleming, Brad, Gabby, Buddy—"

"Yes," said Alex. "Yes, it has killed many. But not all."

"How do you know that?"

"I did my research," she said. "I dug. And I have a nearly complete record of ownership. There's a few missing spots, a couple months, here and there, where I don't know who possessed the book, but for the most part, I have the names, the locations, and the outcomes. And yes, there are many deaths. Most who owned it didn't understand the book. But not all."

Annie paused, letting it sink in. "Someone has solved the mystery?"

"Yes," said Alex. "Multiple someones." She pulled a notebook from a pocket. She gestured toward the counter. "May I?"

"Sure," said Annie, and Alex laid the notebook open. She flipped through pages, and Annie saw neat rows of writing, page after page of notes. Alex flipped back to earlier in the notebook.

"It took roughly two years after Mike Sullivan died for someone to solve it. The early years are the hardest to track, and there are two separate one month periods where I don't know specifically where the book was. But I do know that a Mr. Timothy Harden solved the book, twenty-five months after Mike Sullivan died."

"How do you know that?"

"Well, he's still alive, for one. I tried to contact him, to speak to him, but all my attempts were rebuffed. A lawyer eventually told me to stop or legal action would be pursued."

"Maybe he didn't read the book," said Annie. "He could have owned it, not read it, and then sold it. If only we had done the same."

"I don't think so," said Alex. She flipped a page. "Harden was a carpenter, prior to his ownership of the book. He ran a small carpentry shop in Newark, New Jersey. An honest living, but by all accounts he lived a modest life. Married, a single child, and owned a simple home in the suburbs. After his ownership of the book—well, he wasn't a carpenter anymore."

"What happened to him?"

"He lives on a large estate in New York, and owns multiple properties inside the city. With the mild amount of snooping I did, he seems to own multiple exotic sports cars, plus private jets. Eats at expensive restaurants. Dines with supermodels."

"Supermodels?" asked Annie. "What about his wife? Or his child?"

Alex glanced at her. "I can't find evidence of them."

"What does that mean? Can't find evidence of them?"

"It means that as far as I can tell, they no longer exist. And as far as the state of New York is concerned, Harden isn't married."

"What the fuck does that mean? People don't just disappear."

"This is speculation on my part. But bear with me. Imagine. You're a carpenter in the suburbs of Newark. You work hard, and eke out a living, supporting your small family. You married young, and had a child without planning for it. You consider yourself a good person, a responsible person, and so you work hard, and start a business, and support them. Maybe you're not happy with your life, but you continue on with it the best you can." Alex paused. "And then a book falls into your lap, with a warning and a promise. You read it, and it grants you your heart's deepest wish."

"And your heart's deepest wish is to be rich, successful, and single, with no children."

"Yes," said Alex. "And so the book grants your wish. And so it wipes your wife and child off the map. Erases them. And you are free, and wealthy, and may do whatever you wish."

Annie took a deep breath. "It rewrote reality."

"Yes," said Alex. "It's a frightening proposition, that it has that much power. But honestly, it could be worse."

"How could it be worse? You're telling me Harden potentially used the book to erase his own wife and child from existence."

"It's only one potentiality. Imagine this, instead. That Harden loved his wife and child. That he worked his knuckles to the bone to support them both, and wanted the best life for all of them. Also quite possible. So, when the book found its way to him, and he saw a way out of scratching and clawing, he took it." Alex paused again. "And it worked out. He solved the mystery of the Sentinel Lodge, and the book granted his deepest wish."

"Without his wife and kid?"

Alex shrugged. "I don't know. I don't know how the

mechanism works. Does the book sense what your wish is? Or do you have to wish it specifically? Is it just what you have in mind? But it's not impossible to believe that perhaps Harden wished for extraordinary wealth and an easy life, and assumed that of course that included his family. Why wouldn't it? And perhaps the book granted the wish—"

"And erased his family, to spite him?"

"I don't know," said Alex. "Both are possible."

"Well, at least we know it's possible," said Annie. "Are there others?"

"Yes," said Alex. "Most are a similar story. Mild mannered people come into contact with the book, and suddenly are wealthy and successful."

"Or dead."

"Yes," said Alex. "I don't want to mislead. Most who read the book die. But not all. And that tells me it's a solvable problem."

"Have you spoken to anyone who's solved it?" asked Annie. "Ask them directly how they got to the true ending?"

"No," said Alex. "Not directly. Only through intermediaries. Most have isolated themselves, and at any mention of the book, they cut off contact."

"Why wouldn't they at least talk?"

"It could be many reasons," said Alex. "They faced something difficult, and don't want to be drawn into it again. Easier to cut off contact. Or they're afraid that the wish will be discovered, that their wealth isn't 'real.'"

"I guess," said Annie. "Did you get anything useful from them?"

"Something, perhaps," said Alex. "There was woman who solved the book. A Samantha Thaxton. She sent me a letter through her lawyer. But calling it a letter would be generous. It was a message. Short and sweet."

"What did it say?"

"Sullivan is the mystery." said Alex. "That's it."

"Sullivan is the mystery?" asked Annie. "What the hell does that mean?"

"I have my theories," said Alex. "I'm guessing it lies in the history of Mike Sullivan."

"Is Sullivan in the book?" asked Annie. "Sullivan is the mystery." Annie repeated it in her head, trying to pick it apart.

"It's hard to say," said Alex. "If Sullivan is the mystery, we must solve him, to get to the end of the book. But he is dead, and won't be providing us any answers."

"It's not very helpful."

"I'm not sure anything would be," said Alex. "If the book does indeed reshape itself between readings, what guidance could they give?"

"They could give us a map."

"I've thought about it a lot," said Alex. "And the only definite conclusion I've come to is that some things will be opaque until we've started reading the book. That until you've opened it, your perspective is limited."

"So, any planning is pointless?"

"No," said Alex. "I didn't say that. Have you read any choose your own adventure novels?"

"Plenty as a kid," said Annie. "But none since then."

Alex nodded. "I have every choose your own adventure novel Mike Sullivan wrote. Most were under his pen name, JP Harmon. But there were a handful of others, under different names, and I've hunted them all down, and read them all. More than that, I've quantified all the data. The twists and turns of each book, and how he structured the stories."

"Even when I was a kid, I recognized how formulaic they are."

"Exactly," said Alex. "They don't always follow the same format, but largely, they do. Introduction, with only one path. Then a branch, which offers one apparently safe path, and a dangerous one. The safe path is a ruse, always. So you take the dangerous one, and you get a seemingly random choice, with both of them leading to another branching path, one that leads into danger, and one that leads to safety. Here, the safety isn't a ruse, and is always the safer pick. It's here where more plot points are introduced, followed by another branch, this time with a dangerous choice where you can learn information, or a safer pick, to try and escape."

"The dangerous pick is the correct one, right?"

"It's tricky," said Alex. "Because most of these are consistent within all of the books, and we're talking over fifty of these books. That's a significant enough sample size for me to be confident about it. Consistent meaning over ninety percent of the time. But here, it's much closer to a random choice. Sixty percent of the time, you're right."

"So, a majority."

"Yes, but still, not significant. But I've mapped out the percentages, to find the 'happy ending', as it were. So we have a map, so to speak, even if the book rearranges the pages, it doesn't matter. We can still follow our guidebook."

"I have a question," said Annie. "How do you decide what the happy ending is?"

"It's an important distinction," said Alex. "I always judged it as the best outcome, giving the reader the most happiness. Honestly, it was usually clear cut. I doubt Sullivan would have changed much of anything."

Annie thought over her words. "I'm more concerned if the book has altered the concept of the true ending. Of solving the mystery. What if solving the mystery kills you?"

"We can only prepare for what we know," said Alex. "We can look at my data, and make the best choices."

Annie took a deep breath. "You're right."

"Are you on board?"

"I think so," said Annie. "When do you want to read it?"

"I have two proposals," said Alex. "One, is that we read it at my house. It's safe, and it's isolated. No one will intrude, and no one can steal the book away from us."

"Where do you live?"

"Upstate New York," said Alex. "Four hour drive from here, give or take."

"We just met, and you want me to go to your house, four hours away?" Annie stared at her. Alex seemed to be a straight shooter, but she could be tricking her.

"Removing it from the area keeps it from spreading to anyone else you might know, who would conceivably investigate after our deaths," said Alex.

Annie inhaled through her nose. "Fair point," said Annie. "Wait—*our* deaths? Why would we both die?"

"That leads me to my second proposal," said Alex. "We read the book together."

"Together?" asked Annie. "That seems dangerous. And wouldn't it be smarter for us to split our opportunities? To read it separately, in case the first doesn't make it through?"

"I have my reasoning," said Alex. "I also have a Plan B. We can talk it over on the drive."

20

Sullivan is the mystery.

The four words echoed through Annie's head as they drove to Alex's house, hours away.

She puzzled it out, over and over again.

Can you solve the mystery of the Sentinel Lodge? asked the back cover of the book. A simple question, to drive a reader into the book, to solve the mystery themselves. No different from the covers of hundreds of choose your own adventure novels.

"Sullivan is the mystery," said Annie, she murmured to herself.

"What did you say?" asked Alex, her eyes on the road. 90s alternative played quietly over the car's speakers.

"Sullivan is the mystery," said Annie, louder. "I don't understand. Was this woman just messing with us?"

"It's certainly a possibility," said Alex. "Most of the people who have solved the book didn't reach out at all, so it's hard to know her motives. I asked for clarification, but only got radio silence."

They had talked strategy, with Alex going over in detail the likelihood of each path through the book, and why reading it together would give them better odds. Two people working on the same puzzle exponentially added a higher probability of success. When they came to an impasse, they could talk it out. But the cryptic hint still floated around inside Annie's mind.

"Sullivan is the mystery," said Annie. "Sullivan *wrote* it. I doubt he used a self insert. And yes, writers do put a lot of their identity into any book, but this—it's a choose your own adventure novel."

"We need a perspective shift."

"What does that mean?"

"I just don't think we'll be able to understand," said Alex. "That was the only conclusion I could come to. That anyone who reads the book experiences something that fundamentally changes their perspective."

"I mean, Judy spoke of traveling to the Lodge itself. Of hiding, and hearing her husband be killed."

"I think it's something deeper than that," said Alex. "But it's hard to know what it is. And certainly, Judy's experience was terrifying, but still, so limited. She only heard what Mike went through. What was outside that room? What is in the lodge, if it is indeed there? The woman who sent that hint, she succeeded. She won a wish. Did she simply read a book, get to the end, and boom, her wish was granted?"

"Isn't that what we're aiming for?"

"Yes. It's partially why I want to read together. Because I think the book is only the first part of the puzzle. And we'll need both of us to get through the following parts." Alex stared ahead at the road. "And if it's not enough. There's always Plan B."

"What's Plan B?"

Alex told her.

"Really?" asked Annie. "That's Plan B?"

"It can't hurt."

"I guess not," said Annie. "What about the wish?"

"What about it?"

"We haven't talked about it."

Alex glanced at Annie, her eyes reading her, and then going back to the road, mostly empty at midday. "What we wish for."

"Yes," said Annie, despite Alex not asking a question.

Alex took a deep breath. "It's difficult. Our heart's deepest wish." She paused. "It feels like a trick."

"The book *is* a trick," said Annie. "I thought we agreed."

"Yes," said Alex. "And all of the cursed items have only given with extreme cost. But many of those who've succeeded are still alive, and living well. But I do not know if a genie will pop out and ask us directly—or, perhaps, the book will simply sense our desire, and reshape reality to fit it."

"What we want, versus, what we would wish for, are two different things."

"Truly," said Alex. "But if you're asking me, if I had a choice, or even a suggestion for what we wish for—I would suggest we wish for the book to lose its power. For it to be a simple choose your own adventure book."

"But we could do so much more," said Annie. "Why not wish for the book to never have existed? It would undo so much death, so much tragedy." Annie felt tears well up, the images of Gabby and Buddy's bodies suddenly in front of her eyes.

"It's true," said Alex. "And I know, the death of your friends weighs heavy. But the larger the ask, the more dangerous the results. The book reshapes reality, and if we ask it to erase the book completely—what will the ripple effects be?"

"I want my friends back," said Annie. She wiped away a tear with her sleeve. Heat had risen into her chest, into her face, all the sadness and grief she had swallowed down, returning.

"I know," said Alex. "But there is no part of me that believes that the book will go quietly. If we ask it to erase its sins, I believe it will create new ones in its wake."

Annie took a deep breath, forcing the emotions back down again. "Are you saying we have to be reasonable with our heart's deepest wish?"

"I understand your point," said Alex. "I'm not saying to be reasonable. I'm saying to be smart. Because if you wish for your friends to be alive, the book will twist reality to punish you. And I think that will be true of any wish, except for the one to defang it. Because *that* is the trap. That even if you succeeded, you will only wish selfishly, and therefore continue the book, and propagate more death."

Annie took a deep, harsh breath. It held back the tears. But it also restrained the anger, the intense rage that she had bottled up, the furious feelings of injustice that had burned inside her. It wasn't right, it wasn't fair, and this was the way she could *make* it right, make it fair. She could bring back her friends, and finish this book, this cursed thing, and live a normal life, the one she hadn't cherished as much as she should have only a few short weeks ago.

But Alex was right. Annie knew she was, that being selfless, that choosing to end the book's cursed power was the *right* thing to do, but Annie didn't want to do the right thing. She wanted to save her friend's lives, the thing that *felt* right.

"Look, you don't have to agree with me—"

"No, you're right," said Annie. "But it's not what I want."

"I know," said Alex. "It's not what I want either." Her voice trailed off.

Annie looked at her. Was that emotion from her? A peek at some vulnerability?

"What is it you want?"

"Things with my family to be different," said Alex.

"You mentioned some unpleasantness."

"I did." She lapsed into silence.

"Well?" asked Annie. "What happened?"

"It's not of consequence."

"Of course it's of consequence," she said. "If it's important enough to wish it away. You're risking your life with me, delving into this book and its curse, and I still know nothing about you."

The car fell into a silence, Alex's face struggling.

"I don't like talking about it," Alex said, finally. "It's painful to think about, and will only distract us from our mission."

"I want to trust you, Alex," said Annie. "This is how you establish trust."

"I suppose you're right," she said, her face relenting. She

took a breath. “My parents were quite wealthy. Inherited wealth, industry. My great-grandfather established a presence in mining, and the old money continued onto us. To my grandfather, and to my father. Still a family run business.”

“*Were* quite wealthy,” said Annie. “Not anymore?”

“No.”

“What happened?”

Alex stared ahead, her face still. “My brother happened.”

“The unpleasantness.”

“Yes,” said Alex. “He’s my younger brother, a year younger. Just us two. And my father groomed him from very early on, to take over handling the business. Despite the fact my brother is inept, has no business sense, and has little instinct for it. No leadership abilities. Nothing.”

“You wanted to be there?”

“It’s a difficult question,” said Alex. “I’ll say this. I would have done a good job. I would have steered the company well, and would still be working there today. I would have pivoted the company when necessary. I would have led. But my father told me, in quite clear terms, that it would never happen. That women don’t run the family business. Men only, regardless of ability. My father was given control for the same reason, and he wouldn’t break from tradition. And my brother ran our family name into the ground.”

“What happened?”

“Entropy. A decline, into bankruptcy. My parents, knocked from their high horse. My brother, a public failure. Scandal.” Alex shook her head. “I don’t ask for pity. The loss of generational wealth is only sad to those who lose it. But I took my own path. I survive on my own, now. But it was never about the money, or the power. It was about trust, like you say. About my father not trusting my ability. Or not seeing I was capable."

Alex fell into silence, the radio still playing. Alex reached out and silenced it.

"It doesn't matter anymore," said Alex. "All of it is past. We only have to worry about the book."

*

They got to Alex's house late in the evening.

Alex's house was simple. Annie had imagined the house of a magnate's daughter, but it wasn't any larger than Annie's home. The plot of land it sat on was big, though, and it made the house feel smaller still.

Alex led her through her home, giving her the dime tour. The house was nice inside, tastefully decorated. It seemed slightly sterile, but it matched what she knew of Alex's temperament. She had Fleming's display room in mind, something that showed off his collection. She had imagined something like that for Alex. Annie had assumed incorrectly.

"Are there—" she started.

"Objects here?" asked Alex. She pointed at a curio cabinet, set against the wall. "Right there."

Annie walked over, studying the objects inside the cabinet, through the glass. Simple items. A stuffed teddy bear. An iron. A typewriter. A few dozen of them, arrayed behind the glass.

"I was expecting—"

"Something more ostentatious?"

"I guess."

"I don't have room," Alex said. "I don't keep any of the

larger objects. I'm more willing to bend on price, and it keeps them moving."

"All of these things were cursed?"

"I wouldn't say cursed," said Alex. "I don't think all of them gained power through nefarious intent. Some were accidents. Some intentional. Some inexplicable. But all of them are mundane now."

Annie stared at them. She felt nothing from them. No pull, no gravity. They were just things. Remnants of supernatural power.

"Let me show you the guest bedroom," said Alex. She led her to the guest room, a simple bedroom, sparsely decorated, with a full size bed. "Hope it's okay."

"Looks fine to me," she said. "Tomorrow?"

"Tomorrow," said Alex. "We can have a nice breakfast, first."

Annie nodded.

"If you need anything, just ask. I'll be reading. Don't worry about interrupting."

Annie nodded again, setting her small piece of luggage down. Alex gave her a small, awkward smile, and then shut the door. Annie sat down on the bed. It sagged slightly under her weight, but felt comfortable.

Her purse sat next to her. She spread it open, and pulled the book from it, enclosed in newsprint, crinkling as Annie wrapped her fingers around it.

Her heart caught in her throat just touching it. Clawing tension pulled at her stomach.

She peeled the paper back, looking at the cover again. She examined it, staring at the art, flipping it over, reading the back cover once again. Slide it into the stacks at any used bookstore, and it would disappear.

Annie held the book, and the tears came then, and she didn't stop them. She wept silently.

Brad, Gabby, Buddy. All gone because of this stupid thing, some children's book. She squeezed it, the soft binding bending in her hands.

But it didn't break, no matter how hard she pressed.

She let herself cry, until there was nothing left. Annie grabbed a tissue, wiping her eyes, and blowing her nose. She stared again at the book. A stupid choose your own adventure novel. A novelty. A toy.

Tomorrow.

Tomorrow, they'd solve the mystery of the Sentinel Lodge.

And no matter what, she'd get her friends back.

21

Alex made them a good breakfast. They sat down to read afterward.

Alex pulled two chairs together.

"You really think this is the best way?" asked Annie. "Both of us at the same time?"

"Yes, I think so," said Alex. "Two minds are better than one. We can cover each other's blind spots."

"It's putting all our eggs in one basket."

"Yes, but I believe in this basket," said Alex, cracking a smirk.

"So you are capable of jokes."

"I'm mostly not trying to break into a thousand pieces because of the stress," said Alex, taking a deep breath.

"What's the worst that could happen?"

"Exactly," said Alex. "You ready?"

"I think so," said Annie. She eyed Plan B. "You think that will be necessary?"

"It's Plan B for a reason."

"True."

The book lay between them, the simple, slim paperback unwrapped from the newsprint. Annie grabbed it.

She took a deep breath. Her heart thudded in her chest. She held a grenade in her hand, and they would pull the pin together.

But they would not throw it.

They would hold it in their hands, and hope that it wouldn't explode between their fingers.

Annie picked up the book, and they shimmied their chairs even closer together, their shoulders touching. It was small, and if they would both read it, they would need to be close.

She held it out, between them.

"How are we doing this?" Annie asked.

"Each of us holds it with one hand," said Alex, reaching out to the book. Annie nodded, her heart thudding in her chest. She was going to have a heart attack before they even opened the thing. Annie took another deep breath, holding it for a moment, before letting it out.

"Are you okay?" asked Alex.

"Trying to keep myself calm."

"Easier said than done," said Alex. "Let's get started. You ready?"

"Yes," she said. She took a final breath, and flipped open the book, giving the other edge to Alex. The book laid open there, in front of them.

A title page.

Choose Your Fate: The Mystery of the Sentinel Lodge

Annie took a breath, her heart still beating hard. Her hand shook slightly, and she reached over and turned the page. Normally there would be a copyright page on the left, but there was nothing, only a blank. This was never published, only printed, so Mike didn't bother.

Annie glanced to the right, expecting no dedication either. Why include a dedication in a book never published?

But there was one there.

For Judy, for Sam, for Joanie. For me. If all goes well.

Alex said nothing, taking a breath. Annie flipped the page, ready for the story to begin.

Your breath catches in your lungs as the chill air enters them. You stand outside of the Sentinel Lodge, six stories tall, staring down at you. The Rockies surround you, mountains towering high.

A voice startles you.

"You must be my new assistant caretaker," said the voice, and you turn to see a man who looks to be in his 50s, with graying hair and cold eyes. They are squinted against the glare of the sun off the snowpack.

"I am," you say.

"I'm Carl Douglas," he says, and he extends a hand. You reach out and shake it, his hand big, enveloping yours, and he smiles as he squeezes.

"Nice to meet you," he said. "Follow me inside."

TURN TO PAGE 3

"The intro," said Alex. "No choices. Important details.

Lodge is six stories tall. It's cold, and we're surrounded by the Rockies. Carl is the caretaker, and our boss."

"It's ominous," said Annie.

"Yes," said Alex. "It would be."

Annie turned to page three.

"It's a beautiful hotel, is it not?" asked Carl, as you enter the wooden double doors. You look up to see the elevated ceilings in the lobby, with off-white walls decorated with ornate art, spanning multiple decades and even centuries. Intricate chandeliers hang above you, and for a split-second, you imagine one crashing down on top of you, its many pieces of glass cutting you into a million pieces—

"All original art," said Carl, interrupting your thoughts. Light penetrated through high windows, illuminating the lobby.

Carl continues to show you around, first the lobby, then the maintenance areas, and finally to the grand garden outside, with a massive hedge maze adjacent.

"Take a good look," he says. "We're getting a huge snowfall. After tonight, all of this will be buried."

You follow Carl back into the lodge, where he leads you to your room on the second floor. It's modestly sized, but has everything you need.

"Here's your room," said Carl. "Get settled in, it'll be your home for a few months. I've already taken care of everything today, so you're free to relax. We can get you started working tomorrow."

Carl turns to go, leaving you to your room. He stops at the door.

"One more thing," he said. "Don't leave your room tonight."

"Why?" you ask.

"The lodge—well, it gets a little spooky at night," said Carl, with a half smile. "Unless you know what you're doing, it's best to stay here. Trust me." His smile disappeared. "Stay in your room, and everything will be fine."

He left, leaving you alone.

TURN TO PAGE 5

On page four, an illustration stood, of Carl looming over you, smiling, showing you the grounds of the lodge.

"Still no choices," said Annie.

"Not unusual, early on," said Alex. "Clearly we're not supposed to leave our room, which means we need to leave our room, when the choice is given."

Annie turned the page, and their first split path was on the next. They could stay in their room for the night, or leave, and explore the lodge.

"We leave, right?" asked Annie.

"The 'dangerous' path is always the correct choice," said Alex. "If we stay, we will lose."

They left their room in the lodge, Annie turning the page.

"Left or right?"

"This is random," said Alex. "Go left."

"Page 78," said Annie, and they flipped to it.

They turned left down the hall.

You hear a screeching noise from above you, followed by a horrible wailing. The sound makes your skin crawl, and your hair stand on end. It sounds like someone being killed. Or coming back from the dead.

Below you, you hear a heavy thumping noise. A rhythmic noise, almost like a machine. It gets louder, even as you stand there, pondering your next move. If you pause a moment, you can almost feel the lodge shake from the sound.

TO GO UPSTAIRS TURN TO PAGE 99

TO GO DOWNSTAIRS TURN TO PAGE 45

"Jesus," said Annie. "Which direction do we go?"

"This is random," said Alex. "The next decision is the important one."

"Downstairs, then," said Annie. They turned to page forty-five.

You creep downstairs, peeking around every corner, looking for the source of the noise. You find yourself back in the lobby, completely empty. Carl is nowhere to be seen. The wind swirls outside, the snow billowing across the frosted glass. The thumping noise is only louder now, shaking the very floor you walk on. Whatever causing the noise is impossibly strong.

The noise seems to come from down a hallway, into the staff area of the lodge.

You hear the wail again, distant, above you. You realize you're in terrible danger, and it was an awful mistake to leave your room.

TO FIND THE SOURCE OF THE NOISE TURN TO PAGE 77

TO RETURN TO YOUR ROOM TURN TO PAGE 81

"What's the play?" asked Annie.

"I don't know."

"What do you mean?" asked Annie. "I thought at this

point, safety was the right call."

"It would be, but—" Alex's voice drifted away.

"What is it—" started Annie, but then she saw.

They no longer sat in Alex's house. They were in the Sentinel Lodge. The transformation had been silent and complete. They sat in the lobby, in one of the many armchairs, next to each other.

"We haven't gotten to an ending yet," said Annie.

"I don't know if it matters," said Alex. "We—"

"You left your room, son!" yelled a voice. Carl approached them. He held his axe with love. It was stained with blood.

"Rule number one is not to leave your room at night!"

22

Carl raised his axe, screaming, spittle flying from his mouth.

"You left your room! You left your room!" he yelled.

"Plan B!" yelled Annie.

Alex pulled Plan B from her waistband, and aimed at Carl, pulling the trigger three times.

BANG

BANG

BANG

Three blooms of red opened in Carl's chest, staining his workman's shirt. His scream died in his lungs, and he dropped his axe, thudding to the ground. He stared at the two of them, the inarticulate rage in his eyes vanishing, replaced by an emotion that looked foreign to him.

Surprise.

He didn't expect the pistol, and didn't expect three shots, and the look on his face locked as he died on his feet, and fell to the hardwood floors of the lodge's lobby. Black blood spilled out from underneath him.

They stared at the body of the crazed caretaker.

"Well, I'm glad we brought the gun," said Annie. "We're in the Lodge."

"Yes," said Alex, catching her breath. "We've been transported here."

"We followed all your rules," said Annie. "We made the right choice, every time. We didn't even get an ending!"

"A perspective shift. Sullivan is the mystery," said Alex. She was looking toward the entrance. "It's snowing outside. A blizzard."

"It killed Buddy," said Annie. "The cold. We can't go out there. We'll freeze."

"There's nothing out there," said Alex. "If we truly are inside the world of the book, there's nothing in it outside of the lodge."

"So it's just a void?"

"It's frozen mountains," said Alex. "Maybe forever. We can't escape that way. There is the hedge maze. It's right outside."

"Carl was supposed to kill us."

"Yes," said Alex. "Let's do some reconnaissance."

"The front doors are locked," said Alex. "We could break them down, or go through a window, but then again, it's only cold out there."

"What about the maze?"

"I think we only go outside if we have no other recourse," said Alex.

They explored the first floor.

"You should arm yourself," said Alex.

"With what?"

Alex picked up Carl's axe from the floor, and handed it to her, handle first.

"He's not real," said Annie. "And neither is his axe."

"And yet it has weight. And if it hit us," said Alex. "We would certainly die. How many victims have been found dismembered? Victims of Carl and his axe. The violence that happens here is real. The book makes it so."

Annie took the axe, and held it with both hands, its weight surprising her. Enough to split a log.

Or a skull.

Real or not, it felt good to have the weapon.

They explored the first floor, cutting a wide berth around the corpse of Carl.

"Staircases on either side of the lobby, leading up to the six floors," said Alex.

"Just like the book described," said Annie. Annie walked behind the front desk, examining the logbook, the cashier drawer, the keys.

"None of this is real."

"Looks real to me."

"But there are no names in the guest book," said Annie. "Nothing. It's empty."

"There were no guests in the story."

"Yes, but this guest book goes back to last year," said Annie. "There's nothing."

"Well—" Alex paused. "It's not written into the story, so—"

"So, it's skin deep," said Annie. "Set dressing."

"Right," said Alex. "What keys are back there?"

"Only the keys to 'our' room," said Annie. "I'm taking them."

"Can't hurt," said Alex. Alex peeked into the employee's only area behind the desk.

"Well?"

"Empty," said Alex. "Set dressing, like you said."

"Let's check the lounge," said Annie. They walked through the empty lobby, past Carl, who still laid there, dead. They pushed through the double doors, and a carpeted hallway lay in front of them, a distinct orange-red pattern.

"Guess *The Shining* influence wasn't being hidden," said Alex.

"It's marketing," said Annie. "To be fair, a choose your own adventure set in the Overlook would be a huge selling point to me as a kid. Why hide it?"

"Sullivan is the mystery."

"You're turning into me."

"I'm trying to puzzle my way through it."

"A perspective shift," said Annie. "You said we needed one. Well, we got one."

They walked down the short hallway. Annie listened for anything strange, for screams, howls, any sign of the haunted lodge they now occupied. There was nothing, nothing except the howling winds outside. They reached the double doors, and they opened into the lounge, another cavernous space.

Annie gripped the axe tightly, ready for something, anything—but there was only the deserted lounge of the Sentinel Lodge.

Dozens of chairs sat around period appropriate tables.

Annie rubbed her hand against the fabric of the chairs, one after the other. The fabric was slightly coarse, but cushy. They felt like the chairs she had known in her grandmother's house. But they felt real. There was furniture here. This was decorated.

"There must a scene set in the lounge," said Alex. "Hence why the chairs are here. They're described somewhere in the book."

"Judy described a billiards room," said Annie. "And hiding in a closet."

"The billiards room is over there," said Alex. They walked over, the lodge quiet, and looked inside. The pool table sat in the middle of the room, cues leaning against the wall.

"As expected," said Alex.

"What are we looking for?"

"Sullivan is the mystery."

"Jesus, Alex, enough with it."

"We're gathering evidence," said Alex. "The plural of anecdote is data. And also, to be perfectly honest—"

Alex grabbed a pool cue and smashed it against the ground with a SNAP. It broke in two, and she dropped the piece she still held, next to its twin.

"Christ!"

"I'm waiting."

"Waiting for what?"

"For the book to react," said Alex. "We killed Carl. How will the book react? Will it react at all?"

"It hasn't done anything yet."

"No, not yet," said Alex. "I think we're on the right track."

"Did breaking the pool cue tell you that?"

"No," said Alex. "But it does tell me that it's an actual

pool cue. Not a prop. Just like your axe."

"What's next, then?"

"Sullivan is the mystery," said Alex. "Meaning the book isn't."

"Wait—"

"There is no way to solve the book. There is no right path to choose. No happy ending."

"But you said people did solve it. All those people who got their wishes granted—"

"They all did what we're doing," said Alex. "They all were drawn into the world of the book, and they found their way out."

"Sullivan is the mystery," said Annie. "Well, we're here. What's the next step?"

"We killed Carl, the crazed caretaker," said Alex. "One obstacle, taken care of."

"We're still no closer to getting out of the lodge," said Annie. "We can't even go outside. We'll just freeze—"

Like Buddy—

"No," said Alex. "We don't need to escape the lodge. We need to get through it. Solve its mysteries."

"The lodge isn't the mystery. Sullivan is."

"Then we find Sullivan."

"And that will get us to the ending?"

"Yes."

"You don't sound so sure," said Annie.

"I don't think this will be the last perspective shift," said Alex. "Let's go back to the lobby. There's—"

"—nothing else to see here," finished Annie.

"What was that?"

"What do you mean?"

"You finished my sentence. Are you okay?"

Annie stared at her. "Yeah, I'm—I'm fine. I feel like—"

Like I've been here before. But that's impossible.

Deja vu.

"Annie?"

"I—I'll be fine. Let's keep going."

They returned to the lobby, walking back the way they came. They passed through the double doors, down the short hallway, and out the other set of doors and emerged back into the lobby. It looked exactly the same.

Except for one thing.

"Alex, where's Carl's body?"

The massive amount of blood still lay pooled on the floor, where Alex had shot Carl, and had killed him. But Carl's body was gone.

"He was dead," said Alex. "He wasn't breathing. Wasn't moving."

"Well, he's not here anymore," said Annie. "Either he's alive, or someone took him."

"I don't—"

Alex's words were cut off by the sound of a scream from upstairs, a piercing, shrill noise that cut through Annie, her hair standing on end. The scream echoed through the lodge for ten seconds, and then was cut off with a hellish gargling noise.

"What the hell was that?" asked Annie. "That didn't take Carl's body, did it?"

"I don't think so," said Alex. "But it came from upstairs." Alex looked at her and took a deep breath.

"We have to go up there, don't we?"

"Yes," said Alex. "Sullivan is the mystery. I'm thinking it's all Sullivan. Every ounce of this."

"You still have Plan B, right?"

"Yeah," said Alex. "But I don't think bullets are going to solve every riddle this place throws at us."

23

The wind howled outside, louder than before. Snow pelted the windows. They went upstairs, Alex leading the way, Plan B held out in front of her.

The pistol had been smart. Annie had questioned it, questioned how a real pistol could hurt fictional creations—but Carl died all the same.

They crept, and Annie listened for the horrible, piercing scream, whatever caused it, but it didn't repeat, and they climbed the stairs.

"Are we going room by room?" asked Annie.

"Floor by floor," said Alex. "I think anything more minute will reveal itself to us."

They reached the second floor landing. Annie looked up.

"We could go to the top."

"Thinking linearly won't work here," said Alex. "At least, I don't think it will."

"I agree," said Annie. "But the thought did enter my mind—"

Buddy walked through the cold. The scary man was inside, he had an axe, and he had picked up and read the book, and he thought if he went outside, he'd find his mother. He was so, so cold—

Annie shivered, her teeth chattering, the movement jolting the images from her mind. She was so cold, so cold—

"Annie," said Alex.

"I saw Buddy," said Annie. "He was—"

Mommy, mommy, where are you—

"Annie!" and she was back again. "We have to keep moving."

"He's wandering—he's cold—"

"It's showing us the victims," said Alex. "The ones it's claimed. You have to shut it out."

"How—"

"Focus on your breathing," said Alex.

The image of Buddy shuddering in the cold broke into her mind again, the feeling of absolute, numbing cold, and she took a deep breath, and held it, and thought only of her breath, and did it again.

Only your breath, only your breath, in and out—

"Okay?" asked Alex.

"Yes," she said. "But I don't know if I can keep it going."

"Focus on your feet," she said. "Come on, the second floor."

They left the landing, walking down the long hallway that made up the second floor, with doors on both sides.

Annie breathed, and focused on the floor beneath her feet, and the thoughts of Buddy freezing to death in his own backyard disappeared, vanishing.

"I don't see anything," Alex said. "Maybe the second floor is a dud—"

"We want to play," echoed childish voices, from down the hall.

"What the fuck," said Annie.

"Not a dud," said Alex.

Annie looked down the hall, and saw the children standing there, speaking in unison. They held hands, both wearing play uniforms, stained with mud and dirt. It was a boy and girl, no older than seven, both blonde, staring ahead. Their dirty fingers were clasped together.

"Let's play together," they said, their voices much louder than children could possibly be.

"Fuck that," said Annie.

The children walked forward, strolling at a slow pace.

"What the hell do we do?" murmured Annie. The two children advanced.

"We—"

Eddie wandered through the halls of the hotel, bewildered, confused. His body ached, not ready for the exertion. This wasn't how it was supposed to be, if he read the book, he'd get what he wanted, what he had earned, everything would work out, work out for once—

Annie squeezed her fingernails into her palms, hard enough to cut, and she was back in the Lodge, out of the image of Eddie, who had died hoping he'd be able to build a bookstore, and then they'd bought his books.

Alex stared off into the middle distance, and Annie

shook her by the shoulder, the pistol pointed down at the ground.

"Alex!" she said, stage whispering into her ear, the children still advancing.

"Sorry—" she said, coughing. "Sorry. Lost myself there."

"Are you okay?"

"I'll be fine," she said. The children drew closer. "What do we do?"

"Sullivan is the mystery," said Annie, quietly.

"Yeah, I know—"

"He lost his kids. To an accident. Twins," said Annie. "That's what Judy said."

"That's a mighty big coincidence," said Alex. "Twins, here? Dead, wanting to play?"

"He blamed himself. Sullivan did. Judy said so."

"We can't shoot them," said Alex. "But I don't know—"

"We fix his mistake," said Annie. "He wasn't with them, and they died. We play with them."

"Are you sure?"

"Yes," said Annie. "Violence will only make it worse."

The two kids advanced, holding hands, and as they drew closer, Annie saw more detail. They were more than dirty. They were covered in dirt, and mud, yes, but also in bruises, their bodies beaten. They had been killed, brutally, something destructive.

"Hurting them will only make it worse," she said. "We have to play with them. We have to see what they want us to see."

Annie took a deep breath, her heart thudding against her rib cage, forcing herself to keep her steps steady, and her feet walking. Everything in her told her to turn, to run—or to take the axe and chop down these inhuman things, these things that had once been children, but now were dead, transformed by the lodge, or created by it, empowered by it, to chop them down, to stop them, like they had stopped Carl—

"Do you want to play?" they asked, approaching them. The kids looked up at them, and Annie saw the light in their eyes, and—

They were just kids.

The two children let go of each other, and reached out their hands, the boy to Alex, the girl to Annie.

Annie took a breath and held it, and took the little girl's hand, and—

The two kids walked along the road near Pittsburgh. The neighborhood was quiet, a safe place for kids to go out and play. Judy had worried, she had, but Mike had soothed her nerves. Kids deserved the open space, without supervision. They deserved to play.

Judy had dressed them in their matching uniforms that day. Her mother had given them for Christmas. Judy had taken a picture, the last picture of them, and she had kept it, kept it even after Mike had died, and looked at them, in her silence. Remembering the moment. The moment before she lost them.

The truck was enormous, a massive thing, a dump truck, carrying rock, trying to find a shortcut around a backed up highway.

The driver wasn't drunk, or tired, or stoned.

Just distracted, looking at a map, GPS not a thing, not to a random truck driver, he had a deadline for his load, and he needed to get there on time—

He barely felt the thump.

The kids were in the street, and were destroyed by the massive machine, their bodies pulled under the heavy weight, their bones and organs crushed by it, and the only solace was they felt nothing, dead instantly.

The driver stopped.

He could have kept driving, and washed off his truck after he emptied his load, and no one would have known.

But he stopped, and saw the death, and lost himself.

He found himself again, at the end of a barrel of a shotgun.

Annie woke up to the sound of the gunfire, of the wail of Judy Sullivan, as she ran up to see what remained of the twins, one girl, one boy, destroyed by the truck. Of the silent tears of Mike Sullivan, holding his wife, who screamed in bitter sorrow for hours, until her throat was gone.

Annie stood there, in the second floor of the lodge, her hand outstretched, next to Alex.

"Alex," she said, barely a whisper.

"I'm here."

The two children had vanished, their bodies broken, stained with dirt and blood and grease. Gone.

She took a breath and held it, and let it out.

No more memories. No more images of death. No more children.

"I think that did it," she said.

"Sullivan is the mystery," said Alex.

The piercing wail from upstairs rang through them again, louder.

24

They followed the scream.

It didn't stop, not now, not with the children gone.

It screamed, wailing, a harrowing noise, filled with rage and sorrow. It burrowed into Annie's heart, the sound, filling her with cold, colder than the deathly, eternal frost that lay outside.

But it was a familiar noise.

Judy's wail. As Mike embraced her.

The children were Mike and Judy's kids, dead too soon, a dark tragedy.

The ghostly scream—

"It's Judy Sullivan," said Annie, as they climbed the stairs. She held her axe high again.

"You said you met her," said Alex. "Talked to her. She's

not dead."

"I spoke to the real Judy," said Annie. "Whatever is here—it's not her. It's some creation of Mike's, as he wrote the book—or as he imbued it with its power."

"Or it took her from him," said Alex. "Took his children. Used them in the fiction."

"Either way, whatever's up there isn't her," said Annie. "And who knows what it wants." They climbed up the stairs, toward the screaming. It felt wrong, to go near it, to confront whatever made the sound. Whatever version of Judy that the book had summoned from the ether.

They climbed to the top floor.

The screaming grew louder and louder, an impossible sound, too loud, too carrying to come from a human throat. It filled Annie, the cold, harrowing scream. It seeped into her from the floor, filling her body, her veins, her bones, the hollow in her lungs, the empty vacuum of her mouth and throat, the darkness behind her eyes, the coldness filled her, and she wanted to vomit, to push it out of her, but there was no expelling this chill.

But they continued. Alex walked down the central hallway, on the patterned floor, the bright carpet glaring, growing brighter as they walked, her gun still tucked into her waistband. Annie followed, her eyes looked ahead and behind, on a swivel, but the scream beckoned them.

As they approached the room where the scream emanated, where Judy resided, where she suffered, the sorrow was palpable, a field of melancholy and woe, that filled Annie too, and tears flowed down her cheeks, a tangible darkness filling them, as they waded into the deeper shores of Judy's sadness.

They passed a dozen closed doors, pushing into the screaming pain, a single open door their target, halfway down the hallway, and they pushed through the sadness, through the sorrow, and Annie weighed a thousand pounds, but not from gravity, but from the heavy weight of regret, an accident, a relationship fractured, unforgiven death.

Annie felt the death of Judy's children, the loss of her marriage, of Mike changing, but she also felt the loss of Brad, of Gabby, of Buddy, and of the dozens of others killed by this cursed artifact, reflecting the pain outward, a trap, to capture as much as they could.

Alex's face, wet with tears, betrayed nothing, but she surely felt the same, and they pushed deeper into the hallway, through the harrowing scream, and to the open door.

Judy knelt inside, a figure of grief.

She screamed into the air, her face a mask of contorted skin, a horrible grimace of sadness and despair. The scream did not stop, her eyes a fountain of tears, pouring down onto the floor. Her hands were gripped into the carpet, squeezing hard, fists balled through the fabric, pulling at it, ripping at the reality of this world, pulling at the unfairness of her life. Her back bent, broken even further in this place than in reality.

The volume was deafening, impossibly loud, and Annie shared a glance with Alex, her face filled with pain, covered in tears. It was too loud to speak, but Annie did not need to. Annie threw the axe aside.

She knew what to do. Annie put one hand to Alex's chest, holding her there. She questioned Annie with her eyes, but Annie shook her off.

Annie entered the hotel room, the scream even louder

inside, her feet sinking into the wet carpeting, wet from gallons of tears, and she crept toward Judy.

The wail was louder still, and if Annie did indeed escape from this place, she would suffer from hearing loss.

But she would pay the cost.

She approached Judy, who wailed, who wailed, and Annie knelt next to her, and embraced her. The wail, the sorrow, the icy feelings of sadness and despair, they permeated Annie, filling her, from tip to toe, and she took it in, and felt it deep, and shared in Judy's grief. She felt the sorrow of losing her children, of her husband changing into a monster, of being trapped in her disability.

Annie felt it all, and then the wailing was gone, and Judy had vanished. Annie gasped, as the melancholy was pulled from her, vanishing in an instant, coughing.

The scream was gone, Judy was gone, and Annie was left alone in the hotel room. Alex approached cautiously, walking into the room.

"Are you okay?" she asked.

"Yes," she said. "She only wanted someone to share in her grief. She only wanted comfort." Annie let out a long breath. The hold on her heart felt lighter now.

Alex looked around the room. "There's nothing else here."

"Sullivan is the mystery," said Annie. "What's left? His children. Judy."

"Who's Carl?"

Annie needed to think, only for a moment.

"His father."

"Does this contain all of his demons? What else is there?"

"His writing career? Judy described it as—" Annie

paused.

Of course.

"Annie? As what?"

"A maze."

"The hedge—" and then Alex gasped, all the air driven from her, a terrible sound coming from behind her. She turned, falling to the ground, Alex's eyes locked with Annie's. Alex reached for the gun, but she had no strength.

The axe was buried in her back, and she feebly reached for it, but couldn't reach it.

How—

Carl stood behind Alex. His previous wounds were gone. He stepped up, and pulled the axe from Alex's back with a horrible sucking noise. Alex gasped again, and looked into Annie's eyes, unable to speak. Alex reached for her, grasping for her help.

Carl lifted the axe high above his head and brought it down hard into Alex's back, and Alex's eyes went still. Annie screamed.

"Not that easy," said Carl. "Not that easy. She was soft. Too soft. Not me. Not me." He pulled the axe again from Alex's back.

Annie scrambled backward, around the bed. There was no way out. Carl stood in front of the door, cradling the bloody axe. Alex still reached for her, with a dead hand, her eyes frozen in death.

"No way out," said Carl. "No way out."

He blocked the only exit.

No.

That wasn't true.

The picture window stood behind her. It peered out into

a field of white, disappearing into darkness just beyond the light of the hotel. The hedge maze stood in the distance, dimly lit, silhouetted by snowflakes.

They were on the sixth story. The fall would kill her.

Carl advanced, the axe ready to strike.

"Fuck it," said Annie, picking up a nearby lamp, and breaking the window. The wind and snow howled, filling the room, and she dove out.

25

Annie fell through the cold night air, the snow swirling around her.

Tuck and roll, tuck and roll, tuck and roll—

The words repeated in her mind, it was her only chance, she would tuck and roll, and it would be okay—

She hit the ground with a thud, her body a sack of potatoes. Annie couldn't breathe, the breath driven from her. She was dead, she was sure—

Wait.

She tested her arms, her legs. Her neck. They all moved, if strained. Then she realized, feeling the ground beneath her.

She hadn't hit the ground at all, but had plunged into a snow drift. It had broken her fall, and kept her alive.

Carl.

She pushed all the thoughts away, and scrambled, pushing through the snow, fighting to her feet. He would be downstairs soon, and she wasn't done yet.

The hedge maze, Alex had said, and she was right, the only place they hadn't explored, and surely the mystery lay inside of it.

She kicked away the snow, her hands already going numb, as she scrambled over the white powder, lost, looking for the ground, fighting through the snow and darkness that lay beyond it.

Annie reached, looking for solid ground, and then she found it, a toe touching something hard, and she touched it with both feet, and found the ground again, her head swimming from the fall, and she saw the lodge, rising above her. She blinked hard, trying to force herself back to her senses.

Annie took a deep breath, the cold bracing, and she got her sense of direction again, and saw the hedge maze, the small garden lights illuminating it. The center of the maze, it had to be—

"Not that easy," yelled Carl, standing in the entrance of the lodge. "Not that easy." That's all he said, over and over again, muttering unintelligible nonsense, filled with rage, frothing at the mouth. They had killed him, shot him, but he had come back, had killed Alex—

He paced toward Annie, the axe ready to strike again.

She ran, ran toward the hedge maze, her feet plunging into the growing pile of snow on the ground as it fell around her. Her hands were already numb, and her thin layers of clothes wouldn't keep her warm for long, the cold already seeping in. But still, she had to try. She had to find the center of the hedge maze. The last mystery of the lodge.

Carl stalked behind her, a slow and steady pace, a dark grin on his face, staring at her as she ran. She sprinted toward the hedge maze in the night, looking for the lights that marked its entrance, and she found it, and entered, knowing it could all be a trap, knowing there was only one way in and out, and if there was nothing here, she'd be dooming herself.

Annie ran, she ran, entering the maze, confronted by a choice, right or left, and she blindly chose right, and there was no time to debate, or to decide, Carl was right behind her. Snow dusted everything, and her feet stomped through it as she ran, turning right, left, right, right, left, left, straight ahead, relying only on her best sense of direction. The center of the hedge maze.

Carl yelled from behind her, somewhere, she didn't see him, only heard his voice, screaming for her death—

A dead end. Annie turned, and sprinted away, and took the other turn, and there was Carl, turning a corner, smiling as he saw her, and she ran the other direction, turning again, looking for the way out. She was cold, cold, her chest heaving, sweat freezing on her skin, her hands completely numb, and she stumbled, brushing against the hedge, and it was hard, the sharp ends of the leaves cutting at her.

"This is the end!" yelled Carl. "This is the end!"

He shouted, louder than possible, his voice covering the maze. She couldn't breathe, the cold too much, and she pushed anyway, forcing herself forward.

She darted through the hedges, hitting dead ends, turning back, correcting course. She caught glimpses of Carl, of his axe. Of the bodies of Brad, of Gabby, of Buddy. Of Judy, of the twins. Of Mike.

Annie ran, ran, and there was no center. This maze was endless, without a true solution, without a center. Only a trap, tiring her enough for Carl to catch up, to cut her down, another victim to this book. It was hopeless, and Carl screamed behind her, a bloody inarticulate shout of death and murder, and then she was there.

She stumbled forward into the center of the hedge maze. A fountain stood there, empty, decrepit, snow filling the basin. The fountain had a statue in the middle, of a pen.

A pen?

A fountain pen, golden, and shining, lit, but it made no sense—

She looked around, and saw nothing else. She couldn't breathe, her feet and hands numb, her body cold. She had nothing left to give.

The same fate as everyone else. Killed in this non-space, by this stupid book. She fell to the ground, her lungs screaming. She leaned back against the edge of the fountain.

Carl emerged, a grin still plastered on his face. He carried his axe like a baby, and held it with love, ready to split her open.

"This is the end," he growled, a dark sound emerging from him. He squeezed the handle of the axe, and brought it over his head. Annie watched him as he approached.

She waited.

BOOM

Carl's chest opened, blown apart. Carl fell to the ground, dropping his axe.

How

Mike Sullivan walked around the fountain, carrying a shotgun. He moved with a measured pace. Carl still struggled on the ground, rolling, dark, guttural noises coming from him. Mike stood over him, and pumped the shotgun, pressing the barrel against Carl's head.

He pulled the trigger.

BOOM

Carl's head disappeared. Annie winced, turning away from the gore.

Mike stared down at Carl, taking a deep breath. He walked over to Annie, putting the shotgun down. He extended a hand to her.

Annie looked up, and took it. He pulled her to her feet.

"It always feels good to kill that son of a bitch," he said. "Hi, I'm Mike. I'm the genie in the lamp."

26

"You're Mike Sullivan," said Annie, staring at him. "You're dead."

Mike sat down on the edge of the fountain.

"Yes," he said. "Mostly." He looked at her. "Please, sit down."

"Mike, what is this? What's happening? Why are you here?"

Mike looked around and realized something, nodding. "Yeah, you're right."

Annie blinked, and when she opened her eyes again, they were no longer in the center of the hedge maze. They weren't at the lodge at all. They sat in an office.

A small one, with older furniture. Mike sat at a desk, in a wooden swivel chair, while Annie sat on a nearby loveseat.

The cold, the snow, had been banished, the temperature comfortable. Her aches, her pains, were gone as well.

Annie let out a breath. She looked at Mike. "Did you do that?"

"Yes," he said. "This is my office. Or it was. I'm sure someone else has it now."

"What is this?!?" asked Annie. "Where am I? Did I solve the lodge? What the hell—"

Mike held out a hand. "I'm sorry. I know, it's frustrating. But yes, this is it. The end of the game. The true ending. The mystery of the lodge, the center of the hedge—it leads here. And your wish, if you want it."

Annie took a deep breath. "Are you real? Or are you just another construction of this book?"

"I'm me, as far as I know. I wasn't always here. I remember—I remember life before the book."

She stared at him, trying to read him. Trying to parse what he was saying. And if he believed it. Mike looked as she remembered, from the pictures she had seen. Somewhat older. And something else, too.

He looked tired.

"Why are you here? You're dead."

He shook his head. "I think about it sometimes. This might be Hell. I never believed in it. But you're right. I died, I did. Killed by my own father, in my own damn story. But yet, here I am."

Annie stared at him. "The book put you here?"

"Yeah, yeah, it did. I thought I was clever, you know. After Ellis pitched us on the idea, and showed us it was real—I knew there'd be a trick. I tried to outsmart it. The entity." He shook his head. "It didn't work. I wonder sometimes, if it has a sense of humor. Making me write my own death, over and over—"

"I don't understand," said Annie.

"I created this, Annie." Mike stared at her.

Annie stared back. "How do you know my name?"

"You're in the story, Annie, of course I know your name—"

Annie shook her head. None of this made sense. She stared at him, and heat rose in her chest, a sudden anger.

"You've killed so many. You killed Buddy! He was a kid—"

"Yes," said Mike. He nodded, looking away, solemnly. "I did my part. It's the writer's job. I tried to make it painless—"

Annie wanted to jump out of her chair, to scream, to attack Mike—but it wasn't him. Or was it?

"Judy, your kids—did Mike—the real Mike—did he write them into the story?"

"No," said Mike, looking at her again. "The book used them, to punish me. My dad, too. It's what I get. I paid the price, and I continue to pay it."

"Enough of this. I want my wish."

"Yes," said Mike. "Whatever you desire."

Annie stared at him. "What if I wish the book away? What happens?"

Mike shrugged. "Then it will cease to be. *I* will cease to be."

"There won't be some dark twist, some ironic punishment?"

"I may be the genie, but I don't grant the wishes," said Mike. "I'm the writer. I tell the story. But it always ends the same way."

"Stop talking in circles!" said Annie. "I'm tired of this! I'm tired of puzzles, of riddles, of twists and turns. You killed my friends!" Annie stood now, screaming, yelling. The anger, the rage, it was finally out, after being held back for so long.

"I'm sorry," he said. "I have to say it. I always do."

Annie stared at him, confused.

"You're empty, like everything else here! Another facade, another illusion. That wasn't your children, or your father, or your wife! And whatever you are, you're not Mike!"

Annie felt the smoke bellow from her throat. Tears welled in the corners of her eyes, but she held them back. She wouldn't shed them here, for whatever this was.

"Is that your wish?" asked Mike. "To get rid of the book, once and for all?"

"Will I remember?" asked Annie. "What I wished for?"

"If you want to," said Mike. "Some choose to forget. Some don't."

Annie exhaled. She sat back down, her face in her hands. That was the crux of it. The why of this didn't matter anymore. She had her wish. Alex had told her to get rid of the book, to take its power. It was the only way to win. Every other way only propagated death.

Alex hadn't lost friends. A child hadn't frozen to death under her watch.

And now she was dead, Killed by some facsimile of childhood trauma. By a symbol, a metaphor.

"Do I just say it out loud?" asked Annie.

"You may," said Mike. "Or think it. Picture it in your mind. When you know what you want."

Alex was right. Annie knew she was.

But what if—

Stop it, stop it now.

What if you could have it all? What if you could stop the book, and get your friends back? Undo all the damage?

I can't. It's a trick. It's a trap.

What if it isn't? What if you can make it fair?

No, no—

Buddy's smile flashed through her mind. Of Brad and Gabby embracing. Alex's eyes as Carl cut her down.

It's a trap, Annie. You know it is.

Annie took a deep breath. There was a way out of this. There had to be. She looked at Mike again. He sat, waiting.

Sullivan is the mystery.

He looked tired. Waiting for an answer he already knew.

That's it. That's the way out. Fix everything. It starts with him.

Sullivan is the mystery.

And the solution.

He's *the loophole.*

"I'm ready," she said.

"Are you?" asked Mike, eyeing her. He waited.

She stared at him. "No more games—"

He exhaled, letting out a held breath. "So be it. Your wish is my command."

Annie blinked, and when she opened her eyes, everything had changed.

27

"You ready, Annie?" asked Brad.

Annie gasped. She blinked hard, her heart rate spiking.

"Are you okay?" asked Brad. He sat across from her in a small office. She didn't recognize where they were.

Brad was here. Brad was alive!

"Yeah, I'm— " she started. "I feel like I just woke up from a nightmare." She took a deep breath. She had made her wish. It had dumped her here—

"Are you sure you're okay? I can handle things today, if you're not feeling well."

"No, I'm okay, I just need a second," she said. She looked around the room. It was a nice office. She realized it was *her* office. Framed pictures of her were on the wall. Some with Brad, some of her when she was younger, but others—

But others, well, they were with famous authors.

Stephen King, Neil Gaiman, Colleen Hoover, Janet Evanovich, George RR Martin—

Bestsellers, new and old. And there were more, all over the walls. All stood in front of a sign for their bookstore.

Wait—

"Handle things today?" she asked.

"Yeah," he said. He eyed her. "Are you sure you're okay? We've been planning this for months."

"I—" she started. "Refresh my memory."

Brad looked at her, confused. "Mike Sullivan is on his way from the airport right now. We're the first stop on his book tour. His new book comes out today. Any of this ringing any bells?"

"Oh, right," she said. "Sorry. I don't know what happened to me. Feels like my mind went completely blank."

"There's a thousand people lined up right now, waiting to see him." Brad's phone buzzed. He looked at it. "And he's here. I'll go greet him. How about you take a minute, catch your breath, and meet us out there, okay?"

"Yeah, that sounds good."

Brad got up to leave.

"Brad, wait—"

"Yes?" he asked, in the door.

"How are Gabby and Buddy doing?" she asked, looking into his eyes.

"They're good," he said. "We're all going out to eat later, with Sullivan and his wife and kids. Did you forget that, too?"

Annie smiled. "Of course. I—thank you. I couldn't do this without you."

Brad grinned. "I'm just the pretty face. You're the brains of the operation. I'll go collect Sullivan, and get him set up at his signing table."

Brad left, disappearing out of sight.

Annie took another deep breath. She looked around her office, the office of *her* bookstore, which had hosted dozens of famous authors. Which had thousands lined up outside. Brad, Gabby, and Buddy lived. So did Mike Sullivan, and Judy, and their children.

It had worked.

It had *worked.*

Annie let herself calm down. What she had told Brad hadn't been a lie. She had woken up from a nightmare. Everything that had happened.

Her office phone rang. She looked at the display.

WATSON, ALEX

She answered.

"Hello?"

"Hey, Annie, how's the event going?" asked a familiar voice. It was Alex. She was alive.

"Uhhh, we're just about to get started," she said. "How are you, Alex?"

"Doing well, doing well," she said. "Things are humming along with the franchising. The store in LA just broke ground, and permitting is coming along well in New York. Just got the numbers back in Seattle, for their first month. Gangbusters. It's looking to be a nice feather in the cap for Watson Industries. And for you."

"Great, that's great," said Annie. "I need to go get things organized here. Can I call you back, later?"

"Sure, sure," said Alex. "We need to discuss things, anyway. I'll have Tom schedule something formal with you. Sound good?"

"Yeah, sounds great," she said. "Bye."

Alex hung up. New stores in Seattle, New York, LA—

A distant roar rang out, and she realized it was the crowd, seeing Sullivan. She needed to go out, to greet him.

I don't believe it.

She wanted to pinch herself. Annie stood up and left her office, through the short hallways, toward the roar of the crowd. She exited out of the office area, into the main bookstore.

It was massive, and Annie's heart soared. Stacks and stacks of books. Beautifully organized. It truly was the bookstore of her dreams.

And it was hers.

She walked through the stacks, toward the roar of the crowd. She saw the people, lined up, waiting to get their copy of Sullivan's newest book. To meet him.

Then she saw him, next to Brad. Him and Judy, and the two kids. He was old, much like the version of him in the book. His two children were grown now, as old as Annie.

Judy looked similar, but revitalized. Healthy. And she was standing.

Standing. No wheelchair. No health problems.

"Annie," said Brad. "This is Mike Sullivan."

"Uh—hi. Nice to meet you, in person," said Annie, forcing a smile. This Mike looked the same as the one she had just left, except for his eyes. The weariness in them was gone.

"Same to you, thanks for having me," said Mike. "Honestly, seeing this store in person made it all worthwhile. What a dream. Such a great place to kick off the book tour.

This is my wife Judy, and my children, Sam and Joanie."

The two kids smiled, waving. Judy extended her hand, and Annie shook it.

"Nice to meet you," said Judy. "Something special you've put together here."

"Thank you," said Annie. "It was a lot of blood, sweat, and tears."

"I bet," she said.

"You ready to get started?" asked Brad. "I've got all the copies down there at the end of the table. The customers will grab them there, and then bring them to you."

"Can I see the book?" asked Annie.

"You haven't seen a copy yet?" asked Brad. "I would swear I showed them to you when we got them in. I haven't cracked mine open yet."

"I'm excited about it," said Mike. "It's a little different from anything I've written before. Little bit of a nod to my roots, in choose your own adventure stories."

"What?" asked Annie. Cold rose in her stomach. The memory of Judy's harrowing scream. Of twins, broken by a truck. Carl, carrying an axe.

"When I first started out, I wrote choose your own adventure stories, under a pen name. Eventually got away from it, and well—the rest is history. But this one, well, maybe it's a little self indulgent, but I think I've earned it."

No, no—

Annie hurried to the end of the table, and picked up one of the books.

THIS BOOK IS CURSED was the title. The cover paid homage to the old covers of choose your own adventure books.

"It can't be—"

"I'm really excited to dig in on my copy," said Brad. "The viral marketing stuff got me hook, line, and sinker."

"I didn't go for it, at first," said Mike. "But the kids talked me into it. Said it would help sell the book. And it has. Pre-orders are through the roof!"

"I love the idea of a book that you can't escape!" said Brad. "That you're a character inside the book you're reading! So clever!"

No no no—

Annie picked up the book, flipped through it, towards the middle. She read.

Annie pushed the cap aside, and looked down, the bottom not visible. No one would go down there in the two weeks before it was filled, and afterwards, no one would find it. Not ever.

Annie took a deep breath, and propped her purse on the other side of the cap, and pulled the book out, still wrapped in newsprint. The paper was a little askew, and she pulled it off.

Oh no. No no no.

The book was gone.

Well, not gone.

Replaced.

In its stead was a children's book, slim, of similar size, but for a younger age.

Buddy.

This isn't possible, she'd had her wish—

"It's a fun book," said Mike. "And once I got it in my head, I couldn't think of anything else."

Annie's eyes darted, to the crowd, to her bookstore, to Sullivan, to Brad—

The feelings of deja vu. The familiarity.

"You're in the story, Annie, of course I know your name—"

Annie looked down at the book again. She flipped to the beginning.

Eddie knew now that most of them were filled with mediocre writing that only impressed children, and cliffhanger page turns.

As a child, they were impressive. They were special.

But that wasn't true. He just didn't have access. If they had more money, if they lived closer to a bookstore—he would have seen them all.

This book, though, this one was special. One of one. A modern rarity. The only one printed.

When he joined book collecting circles, people would whisper about this book. In forums, at used bookstores, at antique fairs, and book markets—once in a while you would see chatter about The Mystery of the Sentinel Lodge. One last book, from JP Harmon, before his untimely and gruesome death.

Annie's eyes scanned the page. Eddie. It knew everything. They had gotten the book from Eddie—

But this was the book, but how—

Annie hurriedly flipped to the end

Annie's eyes scanned the last page of the book. It was her, all of it, her entire quest, of finding the book, of her wish, it was all on the page. She couldn't believe it. It was impossible, she had wished for everything to be fixed.

Annie dropped the book on the table, and she screamed, she screamed, she screamed.

How many times?

How many times had she done this? How many times through this story, all repeating, the deaths, over and over—

"Is this real?" asked Annie.

"Annie? Are you alright?" asked Brad.

"I've never been real, have I?" She was yelling now, and the crowd stared at her, the thousands waiting. Brad, Judy, Mike. They all stared.

She tried to think of her life outside—

"There's nothing else," she muttered.

It's all set dressing.

Brad walked to her. "Annie—"

"How did we meet, Brad?"

"What?"

"How did we meet? How did we meet? Why are we friends?"

"We—" started Brad, but his face went blank.

"Was it ever real?" she yelled, at Sullivan. "Tell me. Tell me!"

Sullivan said nothing. He only stared.

Annie dropped the book on the table, and she screamed, she screamed, she screamed.

Enjoy This Book is Cursed?

Sign up here to be notified about Robbie's next novel!

robbiedorman.com/newsletter

And don't forget to leave a review. Reviews are a direct way to help your favorite creators. We appreciate it.

Acknowledgements

Thank you to my wife Kim, for her patience and support, and my team of beta readers: Andrew, Carrie, Matt, Megan, and Yousef. Thank you for reading.

About the Author

Robbie Dorman believes in horror. This Book is Cursed is his fifteenth novel. When not writing, he's podcasting, playing video games, or walking his dog. He lives in Florida with his wife, Kim.

You can follow Robbie on all social media @robbiedorman

His website is robbiedorman.com

Subscribe to his newsletter at robbiedorman.com/newsletter

Milton Keynes UK
Ingram Content Group UK Ltd.
UKHW041646190324
439698UK00019B/238